"That is how to see you—

"That," Amber returned angrily, "is because you're a bully, Alex."

"A bully?" he jeered. "Oh, no, my sweet wanton, I shall not bully you into my bed. I am not so crass. When we make love, it will be because you want me."

"I'd like to know," Amber retorted as calmly as she could, "what gave you the idea that you can whistle me into your bed as though I'm totally without will or strength of mind!"

"As long as your eyes widen each time they rest on me, I know that you want me." Alex lifted her head and smiled into Amber's eyes, hard and confident. "As for strength of will, that, heart of my delight, is what is going to make the next few days so interesting."

ROBYN DONALD, her husband and their two children make their home in the far north of New Zealand where they indulge their love for outdoor life in general and sailing in particular. She keeps a file of clippings, photographs and a diary that, she confides, "is useful in my work as well as for settling family arguments!"

Books by Robyn Donald

Don't miss any of our special offers. Write to us at the following address for information on our newest releases.

Harlequin Reader Service
901 Fuhrmann Blvd., P.O. Box 1397, Buffalo, NY 14240
Canadian address: P.O. Box 603,
Fort Erie, Ont. L2A 5X3

ROBYN DONALD

a late loving

Harlequin Books

TORONTO • NEW YORK • LONDON
AMSTERDAM • PARIS • SYDNEY • HAMBURG
STOCKHOLM • ATHENS • TOKYO • MILAN

Harlequin Presents first edition April 1988
ISBN 0-373-11064-2

Original hardcover edition published in 1987
by Mills & Boon Limited

CHAPTER ONE

THE warm breeze lifted a strand of hair across Amber's face; she blew it from her lips and tucked it back beneath her hat. In the fierce light of a northern New Zealand summer her curls glowed like honey, repeating and emphasising the gold of her skin and the dark warm hue of her eyes, not quite brown, not quite gold. A golden girl, her husband had called her once, long years ago when she was seventeen and a girl indeed.

Strange how wilful memory can be. It was difficult to remember anything pleasant from the time she had spent as Alex's wife, yet she could see his face as he said the words, hear the tender teasing in his deep voice and felt the way her body had quickened in the light of the little sparks which had irradiated the clear grey of his eyes as he spoke that day. Could remember, too, that he had said it without the patronising little smile which usually accompanied his compliments.

Amber sat straight in the saddle, her gaze dark with inchoate fears as it followed the graceful white cruise liner making its way up the channel to its landfall in the tiny port of Opua. She scorned everything the *Kalliste* represented, but each time the liner called at the Bay of Islands she watched its smooth arrival with foreboding and with a light heart saw it go.

For those who had nothing to fear it was a sight worth seeing. The ship, the pride of the Stephanides line, made its way across a sea of blue-green and silver, a molten sheet of colour beneath a brazen sky; around the sleek lovely thing swayed the yachts and launches and runabouts of a water-loving nation. Further along the coast the small tourist town of Paihia was brash and busy, and across the narrow strait was Russell, charming

5

in its old-fashioned appeal but crowded at this time of year when it seemed that almost all of New Zealand came up to the Bay of Islands to bask in the sub-tropical sun.

As it was after Christmas, the flowers of the pohutukawa trees had fallen to carpet the sand beneath them with crimson, but across their dark canopies Amber could see the terracotta tiles of the sprawling homestead roof, almost hidden by a mist of blue jacaranda blossoms. It had been a warm, wet spring, and the grass on the paddocks was green and lush, the animals sleek.

In fact, everything was going so well that Amber's cousin Matt had left his beloved beef and cattle station to take her son on a men-only cruise around the Great Barrier Island, across the width of the Hauraki Gulf. Her generous mouth curved a little as she thought of the postcard which had come in yesterday's mail. Written in Nick's untidy eight-year-old writing, it had announced that he was having a great time, he and Sam Beringer weren't allowed to snorkel by themselves but they had both caught fish for breakfast and he could now dive properly, Sam having taught him.

Matt had been right, as he usually was. Nick was clearly having a wonderful time, not missing her a bit. She had spoken to Arminel Beringer only last night on the telephone, and they had laughed a little wistfully at the ease with which both boys had shrugged off their mothers in the delights of masculine solidarity.

Shivering, suddenly cold in the sizzling air as her brooding eyes followed the liner down the channel, Amber was strangely glad that Nick was not here. The *Kalliste* still had the power to frighten her even though she knew it was irrational. Nine years was a long time, a liftetime . . .

She turned her head away and made a chirruping noise, shaking the reins. The mare was sweet-tempered and docile, and obediently left the delectable tuft of grass

she had been lipping to walk serenely through the herd of
black Aberdeen Angus cattle which were watching
them. Amber swatted at a fly which was hovering
impertinently above her long bare leg and pushed the
Kalliste firmly to the back of her mind.

Almost down to the homestead, they passed the house
of the manager of the beef stud, and his wife. Meri was in
the garden, humming as she played with her baby in the
dense shade of a huge pohutukawa.

'Come and have a cup of tea,' she called, while the
baby laughed and held out his chubby starfish hands for
a ride. 'No, naughty boy, you mustn't cadge rides off
everyone who goes past! You're a real bludger, you little
villain!'

Not in the least abashed, he grinned disarmingly as
Amber dismounted and tied the mare to a post in the
shade of the tree before swinging herself over the fence
and joining them.

'Oh, you're gorgeous,' said Amber, laughing into his
merry face, 'you're just so beautiful I'd like to kidnap you
and keep you for my own.'

He gave her his seraphic beam and sat down hard on
the napkin which was his only clothing.

'If he wakes just once more at three in the morning,
you can have him,' his mother promised grimly.

'I might take you up on that.' Amber scooped him up
and hugged him to her slight breasts, saying, 'Would you
like to come for a ride with Amber, my treasure? On
Amber's horse?'

Peter crowed and clapped his hands. As his mother led
the way into the house she said, 'Don't let him be a
nuisance. If I'd known he was going to beg a ride from
every horse that passed I'd never have let him go with
you that first time.'

'Oh no, Meri, he's a natural. Matt says he's going to be
too big to be a jockey, so he'll be the country's foremost
eventer in twenty-five years' time. Won't you, my lovely
boy?'

The baby thrust a hand through his rich brown curls and gave an impatient thump on Amber's chest. 'OK, honeybun, we'll have a nice cup of tea with Mummy and then I'll take you off. All right?'

It was clear that Peter would have preferred to forgo the preliminaries, but he was as sunny-natured as he was beautiful, so he gave both women a wide, toothy grin and submitted to Amber's cuddling with a good grace.

Meri watched them both with laughter and a faint sympathy in her eyes. Amber knew it was there, just as she knew the other woman would never say anything about the fact that Amber, who adored children, had only one of her own and no prospect of ever having another. Sometimes she ached with the unfairness of it, but she had long ago disciplined herself to a lack of self-pity. There was nothing else to be done. If she wanted more children she would have to divorce her husband so that she could marry again, and she could never do that, because then he would find out where she was.

Just occasionally she had read an article speculating on the reason for his obstinate refusal to marry again, usually coupled with sly references to his spectacular stable of mistresses, and she would shiver. She knew him far too well to believe that he hadn't divorced her because he still wanted her. If Alex ever found her he wanted to be in a position of power so that he could exact the most exquisite of revenges.

But only if he found her. And even he, with all the resources he could command, had not been able to do that. She had hidden her tracks too well.

'Heard anything from Matt and Nick yet?'

Amber welcomed the interruption to her thoughts. 'A postcard from Nick,' she said cheerfully, 'making it brutally obvious he isn't missing me at all. Snorkelling and fishing and sailing are more than enough to take his mind off the fact that this is the first time he's been away from his mother for any length of time!'

Both women traded glances wry with the knowledge

that the independence of sons, though necessary and desired, was nevertheless a little sad.

'When are they coming back? Rod said you told him they'd be a little longer than they planned.'

Amber chuckled. 'Of course, Matt isn't really convinced that the place can function without him, but I was talking to Arminel Beringer on the phone last night and she said Kyle intends to stay away for about three weeks. Like Matt, he needs a rest.'

Meri nodded. 'Matt works far too hard, he needs a decent holiday, so I hope he manages the three weeks.'

'He hasn't had a holiday free from business overtones since I came here, except for the odd weekend skiing. Nine years!'

Amber had lived with her cousin for nine years. And for all that time almost everyone who knew them assumed them to be lovers. Meri was one of the few who didn't.

Handing the baby a rusk, the younger woman said cheerfully, 'I wouldn't worry, these tough men can go on for ever. He'll ease up when he acquires a wife.'

'Matt? My cousin, the one who feels that his empire will crumble if he spends a day away from it?' Amber grinned. 'Of course, if he ever falls in love, there's no telling what the man might do! Unfortunately, I shan't see it. When he marries I'll go, in spite of what Matt says. No woman should be expected to share her house.'

Both women were silent a moment, contemplating the short-sightedness of even the most hardheaded men. Then Meri said thoughtfully, 'Well, he's got a point. It's a huge house, there's plenty of room for you, it would be a shame if you had to go. Nick loves it here, and so do you.'

'It wouldn't work.' The words were expelled on a little hiss, stark and so uncompromising that Meri was startled. Amber bit her lip, hesitating, then finished quietly, 'I tried it once. Isn't the Chinese symbol for trouble two women under one roof? How right they are!' Her hand on the baby's warm little head trembled.

'Ah well, don't borrow it, Matt shows no signs of losing his bachelor status yet. Petey, no, just wait until Amber's finished her tea!'

The baby sat down suddenly and opened his mouth to wail, but the arrival of the cat brought a beam of pleasure to his round little face. Chuckling, he crawled busily across the floor towards it.

'Come and see the weaving I'm doing,' Meri suggested. 'My mother must think I've got unlimited time on my hands, she wants enough material to make a three-piece suit for my father!'

It was, Amber thought gratefully as she admired the superbly subtle pattern on the big loom, a pleasant way of changing the subject. Slowly she relaxed; the stress which her sighting of the cruise liner had caused began to ease. Somehow the rest of the afternoon ran through her hands like a skein of silk, so that it was almost two hours later when she said, 'I'd better get back before they begin to wonder at the homestead whether I've fallen over a cliff. Ready for your ride, Peter?'

'Sure you want him to go?'

'You know I love taking him.'

Peter certainly enjoyed going with her. As his mother handed him up he laughed out loud and wriggled down comfortably on to the horse. Amber's long fingers held him securely across his chest; she smiled and winked at Meri before clucking at the mare.

She would not have taken him out on any more skittish horse, but the mare was placid and accustomed to children, and she seemed to enjoy having Peter on her back, twitching her ears back as his laughter bubbled out through the hot air. Amber turned her head towards the horse paddock, deciding to ride up and let Delight go, then walk Pete back to his mother.

The sun beat down on the checked cotton shirt which protected her shoulders, its hard clarity setting fire to the tossed curls escaping from beneath her hat. A little smile curved the soft full line of her mouth so that she looked much younger than her twenty-six years, no more than a child herself in the brief blue shorts which revealed the slender honey-coloured length of her legs.

She began to sing, a cheerful little tune that Peter loved, and the smile grew as she heard his babbling attempts to join in. At that moment she was truly happy.

Just when she heard the first faint throbbing of the helicopter she wasn't aware. Perhaps it wasn't until the mare twitched her ears in its direction, or Peter turned a rapt little face southwards, his eyes squinting as he tried to pick it out in the blazing sky.

'I think it might be going to fly over us,' said Amber, smiling reminiscently, because Nick too adored helicopters. 'Yes—look, darling, here it comes!'

She halted the mare in the shade of a broad totara tree, competent hands holding both the horse and the baby still, then frowned as the chopper pulled in low and dangerously fast over a woodlot of pines and eucalypts. Whoever was piloting the thing was behaving like a brash cowboy flaunting his skill at a rodeo.

The noise seemed to fill the air. Delight tossed her head but stood her ground; helicopters were not unknown to her. Peter stopped wriggling and stared, eyes and mouth opened to their widest extent as the red and white chopper pirouetted, then settled down no more than a hundred yards away. The engine was cut; the rotors began to wind down, and Amber was suddenly conscious that as she was the only Duncan on the place it was up to her to meet the visitors.

Still frowning, she urged the mare into the sunlight, blinking a little when two men jumped down from the machine. One was the pilot; he waited beside the bubble as the other strode across the lush grass towards her.

She recognised him, of course she did. Only one man had walked like that, as though the world was his, and he free to prey upon it. Only one man had the lean, predatory body, hair black as murder, the arrogant, piratical beauty of feature and form which belied the coldness of the brilliant mind behind it.

Alex Stephanides.

Her husband and the father of her son, the son he did not know he had.

Sick terror held her paralysed until he was only twenty or so yards away, so close that she saw the sun flash in his cruel smile. Before she came to herself Peter let out a whimpering cry and for the first time in her well-behaved life Delight reared.

What followed was a sudden, short nightmare. Amber fought to control the frightened horse with one hand and her legs and her voice, the other hand splayed across Peter's chest, holding his warm firm little body clamped in a steel grip. It was as well that he seemed to have the instinct to ride born in him. He relaxed against her, allowing her to put all her mind and skill to countering Delight's antics. Fortunately the innate sweetness of the mare's temperament enabled her rider to re-establish mastery almost immediately; within a few seconds she had brought her to a trembling, fretting stop.

'Give the child to me.' The deep, almost unaccented voice was harsh with command.

Numbly, feeling like a traitor, Amber obeyed, handing a startled, resistant Peter down before dismounting herself. Alex quelled the baby's rejection with the smooth competence he brought to everything in his life while Amber leant against the horse's damp shoulder, white and shaken, drawing deep breaths into her lungs, her pulse gone crazy in her ears and every bone in her body malleable as dough.

It seemed like an age before she recovered enough to insist, 'I'll take him.'

Another voice interrupted, speaking rapid Greek. Alex answered in a curt sentence and the pilot turned and went back to the chopper, but not before casting a curious glance at the woman who still shivered as if she had a fever. Peter stared goggle-eyed up into the harshly etched features of the man who held him, then essayed a tentative beguiling baby smile.

It was not returned. Alex Stephanides looked at his wife, his expression so murderous that she cried out, then he spat in the soft voice of ultimate fury, 'Whore!' And when she gasped and took a trembling step away from him he smiled as Ulysses might have smiled when he killed his wife's suitors, and went on, 'Is this yet another son fathered on you by your lover?'

Peter began to whimper and Amber recovered herself enough to say huskily, 'You're frightening him, damn you!'

For the first time Alex looked down into the bewildered little face lifted to his. The terrifying fury altered, eased into a mask; he thrust the baby towards her, commanding blackly, 'Take him.'

She turned away, cuddling the child as she forced her sluggish brain to work. Only one thing came through. Dangerous though it might be to claim Peter as her own, it could well be even more dangerous to tell the truth. Whatever the reason Alex had arrived here, it was not for her well-being; the only shield she had against him was the fact that like most Greeks, he loved children and would not willingly hurt one.

Looking down into the round, flushed cheeks of the child burying his face in her breast, she thought half-hysterically that he was a small and flimsy defence indeed.

Aloud, her face still averted, she asked, 'What do you want?'

'You, of course.' He sounded bored, but she was in no danger of misinterpreting this; as many had discovered, when Alex Stephanides sounded his most languid and world-weary he was at his most lethal.

The warm sun could raise no heat on Amber's skin now. Ice stabbed through her body. She wanted nothing more than to shudder, but her will held her upright and calm. 'A pity you came all this way,' she said, forcing a hard, confident note into her voice. 'I have nothing to say to you. Unless you want a divorce.'

His smile made the blood drain from her heart. 'No, I do not want a divorce. Not yet. And I think, my dear wife, that you will find that you have much to say to me. In fact, I am looking forward very much to hearing your voice as you plead with me.'

'I'll see you in hell first!'

His hand closed cruelly hard on her shoulder. 'Oh, no,' he promised easily, 'it is you who will go to hell, Amber. And only when you have broken under the pain of it will I let you go free. Then you will be able to come back to your sons and your lover. If he still wants you when I have finished with you.'

He lifted his hand away as though to touch her dirtied it.

Amber's blood ran cold, but she said steadily, 'You're talking through a hole in your head and you know it. You can't force me to go with you——'

'How much do you love this cousin who is also your lover, this Matt Duncan?'

His softly snarled interruption brought her head up sharply. Slowly she turned, her eyes seeking his above the baby's soft curls. He was still smiling, but the cruelly sculptured line of his lips made a mockery of laughter. Beneath long thick lashes his grey eyes were as cold as death, and as implacable.

'What—has that to do with anything?' she asked, from the depths of a dread she had thought impossible.

Alex's hand stretched out to touch the dark curls above Peter's face, still hidden in her breast. Her pulse leapt and then slowed, sluggish with foreboding.

'You bear handsome children, strong, vigorous. I have seen a photograph of the older boy; he looks very like you. This one looks only like himself. No doubt you wish them both to inherit from their father. He owns much, doesn't he? This station, other farms, orchards. Extensive interests in both agriculture and industry. I could make that heritage—nothing!'

Amber said nothing while he pulled gently on a curl, then released it to watch with dispassionate eyes as it coiled back against the baby's hot little head. That disdainful hand moved to her temple, fingered a heavy honey-coloured lock until the sweat sprang out across her brow. He smiled and his hand fell away as he stepped back and continued in the softest of voices, 'When I have had my fill of your meretricious charms I will consider the debt paid.'

'You couldn't—you can't make me go with you,' she breathed, appalled.

'You must know that there is very little I cannot do! Money and power are all that are necessary for me to bankrupt this cousin whose bed you share, who has given you two sons. I can make sure that he never earns another penny in this life. And he will know why! How much will he love you then, this big, confident, proud man? I can see to it that your children do not——'

'This is New Zealand,' she whispered, sickened by the naked barbaric bludgeon of his power. 'You can't do that sort of thing here.'

Alex laughed, an ugly sound which made Peter stiffen and cast him a terrified glance. 'I can do that sort of thing anywhere,' he stated with such total confidence that she had to believe him.

Amber's brain seemed to seize. She didn't know what to do. The only bright spot in this awful situation was that Alex had no idea that Nick was his son. For a fleeting moment she wished Matt was here to help her and protect her, but she soon banished that. In the short months of that ill-fated marriage Alex had shown sufficient ruthlessness for her to know that he didn't make threats lightly. He was head of the Stephanides Corporation; his power was by most standards virtually unlimited. If he said that he could reduce Matt to poverty, then he could.

And would.

Carefully, in a voice that was flat with the effort to

keep it under control, she asked, 'So just what do I have to endure in this—hell? And for how long?'

The cold satisfaction in his eyes bruised her like a blow. He had expected her to submit. Few defied Alex Stephanides; he was not accustomed to resistance from any man—or any woman.

Yet she thought she saw disappointment darken the ice-grey depths of his eyes before he told her calmly, 'Only for a little while, it should not take me long to tire of you. Certainly no more than the three weeks your lover intends to spend sailing with the bastard son he fathered on you. We shall enjoy a passionate holiday together and then I need never see you again.'

'My God!' she whispered, horrified. 'You arrogant swine! Do you expect me to go to bed with you just like that? As if I were one of your women?'

His eyes narrowed. 'But you are one of my women,' he said starkly. 'My wife. You could have had my respect, an assured position in my life, my children. You chose to throw it all back in my face. So now you will get only what I choose to give you, what I would give a mistress.'

Amber could have screamed with frustration and rage and fear. Her body seemed to tremble with the force of her emotions, but she held tightly on to Peter's little form and returned as calmly as she could, 'Hardly.' And when his straight black brows lifted she enlarged, 'I've always presumed that they at least had a choice. Or do you have to blackmail them into your bed too?'

He smiled, that archaic, humourless smile seen on the old Greek statues. 'Oh, they have a choice. Believe me when I say that I have never in my life taken an unwilling woman. And I will not force you. Your sort of woman is easy to arouse. You were very responsive nine years ago. How old were you when we married? Seventeen. A sweet, passionate little schoolgirl, all innocence and enthusiasm and shyness, and with a child's selfish demands to be the centre of attention. It took only five months for you to become bored with the realities of marriage. Perhaps that was too short a time for you to have discovered that I hold on to my possessions until I tire of them.'

'And so you want revenge,' she said slowly.

'Perhaps. or perhaps I want to know whether your lover has taught you anything in the years since last I had you.'

His misapprehension nauseated her, but she had to admit that it was understandable. Matt was a handsome forceful man, and they lived in the same house. That they were cousins didn't seem to make any difference to the gossip, nor did the fact that, although discreet, Matt had affairs. At first Amber had hated the persistent, inevitable rumours which cast her in the role of Matt's mistress, but as the years went by she had made friends who accepted that she and Matt felt no more than a cousinly love for each other, and most of the time she managed to forget what others thought.

And she had to admit that she was glad that most people assumed that her son was Matt's; such an assumption was an added protection against Nick's real father.

She would always love Matt, because he had welcomed a distraught, unknown cousin without demur, taking her in even although she had explained that if Alex found out he could be dangerous, even when she had to confess her pregnancy. Matt had not hesitated. He knew that if Alex ever found out he would have one of the most powerful men in the world as his enemy, but he had not considered turning her away, he had made her feel that she was wanted and needed and loved.

Thank God her mother had defied her husband's instructions and kept in touch with his cousin in spite of the bad blood between them. Matt was, she told the young Amber only a few months before the heart attack which killed her, the only relation Amber had, and she should not forget his existence.

Unspoken had been the intimation that it was to be a

secret kept from her father who had been ruthless enough
to cut his New Zealand cousin so definitely from his life
that it had taken nine long years for Alex's bounty
hunters to make the connection.

Desperately she said, 'That's obscene. I thought
chastity was important to you——'

'In my wife, of course, but in a mistress it is a distinct
disadvantage.' Alex watched the colour flame across her
cheek and smiled with sardonic enjoyment. 'In a mistress
one wants experience, and an inventive lack of inhibi-
tion. You must have learned that from this cousin lover
of yours, for you were in his bed immediately you arrived
here. The child was born only ten months after the last
night we made love.'

Weak with relief, Amber buried her face in Peter's
curls. Thank God a combination of jetlag and exhaustion
had blotted out of Alex's mind the very last time he had
taken her, in her father's house in London the night
before she had fled from England and a marriage that
had become unbearable.

And thank God Nick favoured the Duncan side of the
family. Apart from the grey of his eyes there was nothing
to connect him with his Greek father. Amber blessed
every individual one of the genes which had worked in
her favour, giving her son the leonine golden splendour
which made everyone who saw them together assume
that he was Matt's child.

Peter began to wriggle and she looked down at him,
her thin brows drawn together. 'Hey, baby,' she said
softly, an automatic, reassuring little smile coaxing an
answer from him. 'Give Amber a smile, now. We're
going home——'

'You have a housekeeper.'

It was a statement, not a question. Amber felt
smirched by the fact that someone had been spying on
her. 'So?' she asked haughtily, without looking at him.

'So we will take the child to the house and then you and
I will leave.'

'Now wait a minute——'

He stepped closer, pinning her against Delight's warm shoulder; she looked into a face harsh with control except for the savage determination in his eyes.

'I have waited nine years,' he said between his teeth, 'I will wait no longer. I accept that you are a good mother, but I do not wish to take your child with us. My plans for you do not allow for your attention to be on any other person but me. So you will leave him with this housekeeper.'

'Amber!' Meri's voice, tentative and a little alarmed, came from behind. The baby gave a great leap and held out his hands to his mother.

Alex swung on his heel and after a quick stabbing appraisal of Peter's mother looked back at Amber with knowledge in his eyes, knowledge overlaid with contempt. 'Liar,' he gritted beneath his breath.

Amber ignored the savage imprecation as she held a chuckling Peter out to his mother. 'I'm afraid he got a little more than he bargained for this time! I couldn't control Delight when the chopper landed and she reared.' She was babbling, the words running freely and thoughtlessly from her tongue.

'Oh lord!' Meri grabbed the boy, hugging him tightly to her.

Alex intervened smoothly, 'Rest assured he enjoyed it! I was watching, and there was no fear on his face.' He cast a sardonic glance at Amber's strained expression and held out a hand, saying with smooth charm, 'I am Alexis Stephanides, Amber's husband.'

Poor Meri gulped, but recovered quickly, putting her hand into his, only to be taken aback as he lifted her fingers to his mouth. Sheer rage held Amber rigid; she remembered only too well that specious charm, the way his eyes gleamed as he kissed a woman's hand, making her feel that she was being wooed with romantic courtliness.

A flush covered Meri's cheekbones; she cast a

harassed glance at Amber's stony face and said hastily, 'How do you do. Are—are you staying long, Mr Stephanides?'

'Alas, only a few minutes. I have come to carry Amber off with me for several days, and we must leave immediately.'

Meri gasped but persisted bravely, 'I see. Where are you going?'

He smiled, the steel momentarily submerged by quick mischief, so disarming it was difficult to believe that it was just as much part of his armoury as his formidable charm and the temper which terrorised his associates. 'On a second honeymoon,' he said outrageously, half-closed eyes watchful above a smile which dared either woman to object.

Warmed by Meri's partisanship, Amber said slowly, 'Don't tease, Alex.' She looked at him, met the warning in his face without flinching. He had the power to make life impossible for Rod and Meri too. Reluctantly she went on, 'Meri came here before I did, she knows very well that we haven't lived together for nine years. We have things to discuss, Meri.'

He was angry, but he said nothing, only held her gaze a fraction longer, the implied threat ugly in its nakedness. Meri nodded, her eyes going from one to the other, still uneasy.

'How long do you plan to be away?' she asked, hugging Peter to her as if to give her courage.

Alex said quite gently, 'I do not consider that to be any of your business. However, if it will ease your fears, I am not in the habit of murdering people. When Amber and I have finished our business together I shall return her here. With no bruises, quite unharmed.'

When he spoke like that nobody dared press the subject. Meri stepped back. She gave Amber a shocked, commiserating glance but retained enough courage to ask, 'And what do we tell Matt if he wants to contact you?'

'Say nothing!' Alexis's brows drew tightly together when Meri looked at Amber appealingly.

It took a strength Amber had to summon from deep inside her to say calmly, 'If the occasion arises, don't bother him. I'll tell him about it when he gets back. However, if there's an emergency, if you have to contact me . . .' She turned to Alex, her expression calm. 'How can Meri get in touch?'

He stared blackly at her before admitting the sense of her unspoken demand. With sharp incisive movements he took a notebook from his pocket and used a slim gold pen to scribble something on a page which he tore out and proffered to Meri. 'That is the number of my office in Auckland. Ask for Mr Leeson. He will know how to contact us.'

Peter began to fuss a little and Amber said with a serenity she was far from feeling, 'I'll see you when I get back. 'Bye.'

Meri bit her lip, her eyes travelling uneasily from the granite beauty of Alex's face to Amber's small valiant one, paler beneath its crown of golden amber hair. With dignity she said, 'Try and have a holiday, Amber. Goodbye, Mr Stephanides,' and left them facing each other like enemies.

'So,' Alex said coolly. 'Come, it is time to go.'

Anger was the only way to suppress the fear. Amber welcomed the emotion, freeing it from the bonds of her normal restraint. 'Are you crazy? I'll have to get some clothes and tell Jane Crawford, the housekeeper, that I'm going. And——'

He silenced her with a caustic smile. 'You will not need clothes. I have provided you with what you will need. And I do not remember that telling people when you are leaving was ever one of your strong points.'

She said bleakly, 'But I'm not running away from here.'

'No, that is so. However, I feel sure that the charming and very pretty Meri will inform the housekeeper that you have gone, and with whom.'

'I have to take Delight back to the horse paddock,' said Amber.

He looked at her with merciless contempt. 'I am glad to see that the years have produced some sense of responsibility in you, but I am sure that someone will see to her as soon as it is learned that you are gone. However, if it will appease whatever conscience you retain, you may take off her harness.'

He realised, of course, that she was snatching at straws to delay their departure. And he knew the reason. Fear. Black, primitive fear, kicking her in the stomach with its power and potency. He was watching her with a hard enjoyment, his arrogant smile pulling at the corners of his mouth because her fear was what he wanted, it fed his ego.

And even knowing that, she was unable to control it. Numbly she removed the saddle and carried it across to the fence, hoisting it up on to a post. Alex made no effort to help her, but stood with hands thrust into the pockets of his well-cut trousers, watching her with aloof and mocking detachment as though she were a servant.

Her skin prickled, but she kept her expression as serene as she could, refusing to look his way as she slid the bridle down the aristocratic nose of the mare and slung it on top of the saddle. Delight whickered and put her nose out to be scratched before walking away, swishing her long tail against flies.

Amber stood with unseeing eyes following after the horse, her mind racing in circles until he said softly, 'Why did you pretend the child was yours?'

'I didn't have much of a chance to deny it,' she returned wearily. And then, although she knew it was hopeless, 'Alex, can't we talk this over like sensible people?'

He smiled coldly. 'I told you that you would plead with me,' he said without expression. 'No, we cannot talk this over like sensible people. Perhaps you are sensible, no doubt your lover is, but I am Greek, and one thing we Greeks understand is revenge.'

'And hubris,' she said hopelessly.

'If overweening pride brings its own reward, then so be it. I shall at least have the satisfaction of knowing that you will have paid your debt to me.'

She paled, but forced herself to hide the desperation in her with an unemotional voice. 'I see. I have your word on that?'

He nodded, watching her keenly. She was looking at the ground, her head bent in almost a defeated fashion, but at that moment she looked up at him, her warm golden eyes suddenly piercing. After a tense second she inclined her head. 'Very well.'

As if she had surprised him, he asked ironically, 'You trust me?'

She was astonished herself at her own conviction. 'Yes. If you give me your word that my going with you will wipe out what you see as a debt, I believe you.'

His mouth twisted, whether at her naïveté or his own darker thoughts she couldn't discern, but all he said was, 'Then let us go, Kostas has waited long enough.'

Amber remembered Kostas. Nine years ago he had been a boy, with the quick-eyed vital attraction of his race; he had matured into a handsome man. She smiled at him, but although he nodded back there was no warmth in his face and she thought she saw insolence in his eyes before he turned them towards the instrument panel. Sighing, but not surprised, she hauled herself up into the helicopter and fell into a seat, her fingers trembling as she fastened the safety belt.

Later she was to realise that it was shock which had made it so easy for Alex to kidnap her. Shock and a deep-rooted primeval terror which had kept her silent when she should have screamed, made her follow him as resistlessly as sheep follow the Judas into the pens at an abattoir.

Later it was easy to wonder if there was something she

could have done; threatened Alex with publicity, perhaps—he hated publicity. But no, she had let him carry her off like a piece of plunder and made no attempt to get away. Perhaps subconsciously she had expected this, known that he was too Greek, too implacable to ever give up the search for the wife who had deserted him. Revenge was a necessity, the desire for it a part of the framework of his character.

Beneath the conscious levels of her mind she must have accepted that, prepared herself for it, and that knowledge had weakened her will to resist.

The helicopter rose above the trees in the woodlot, swooped across farmland and, still rising, sped out over the coast and the sparkling waters of the bay. She half expected it to head towards the *Kalliste*, but it went on over the little settlement at Tapeka Point with its two beaches and steep terraced headland and then out over islands and the glittering sparkling mockery of the Bay, heading towards the wild fastnesses of Cape Brett and Piercy Island until it reached a small island.

Amber remembered it. Unlike all of the other islands in the Bay, it had never been cut over, so it was still covered in trees, mostly tall manuka scrub, but in the centre were remnants of the old forest cover. It had changed hands a few months ago, and the local newspaper had speculated about the new ownership.

But with all the clout at his command, Alex had been able to keep his name out of the dealings. He must have known then where she was, been plotting this revenge while she had been going about her life, happily unaware. The knowledge that she had been watched, every movement charted by impersonally prying eyes, brought her out in a cold sweat. More than anything else it made her afraid.

She sat tensely as they came down on a small landing area cut out from the scrub not very far from the only building on the island, a house which had been built above a curling, pale pink bay facing north and west towards the mainland.

Alexis turned as the skids touched earth; he jumped down with the lithe economy of movement which was a characteristic and reached for her, his hands biting into her narrow waist as he half dragged her out of the machine. Ducking to avoid the rotors, she was pulled into the shade of the trees; the chopper rose, and was gone, leaving only the rapidly diminishing throb of its engine to mark is presence.

'Welcome back,' said Alex, and his dark head swooped and she was kissed with a savage demand which hurt her mouth and stretched her neck intolerably.

CHAPTER TWO

THE SOUND in her ears had to be cicadas, Amber thought dazedly as she stood passive in Alex's embrace. The high-pitched zithering went on and on and on, tearing its way through her hard-won composure, screaming across her nerve ends until she was as strung up as a wire fence.

He was relentless, his mouth imposing a reign of terror on hers, crushing its softness beneath the scourge of his anger. She gave no resistance, standing with eyes wide open, unfocused, as her senses rediscovered all that the years apart had dimmed. He was hard and warm against her, with a clean, faintly salty scent, arousing in its masculinity.

When at last the assault ended she tried to turn her head away, but he ordered, 'Look at me,' and slowly she lifted her eyes and stared into his face. She would have felt safer if he had looked as though he wanted her, but Alex had always been able to subdue his passions to his will, and now was no exception. The clear grey eyes he had given to his son were smoky and turbulent, but he was smiling faintly, and the smile promised not the delights of the flesh, but the pains of hell.

'You are not afraid of me,' he said, almost with satisfaction, a long finger moving gently across her tender mouth in a caress as gentle as the kiss had been violent. 'You have changed. The child I married would be weeping by now, pleading for mercy.'

Her expression remained steady and serene, warm amber eyes remote. 'Is that what you want? Nine years, Alex, is a long time, plenty of time to grow up. I'm no longer an emotional little schoolgirl, bitterly unhappy because the world doesn't live up to my romantic expectations. If part of this revenge you've planned so carefully is to have me pleading for mercy, you're out of luck.'

'No matter. At first I used to imagine it, you know—you begging me to let you go, and then, when I rejected you, pleading with me to allow you to stay. On my terms, because you wanted me beyond madness.' He stopped, his mouth tightening as he watched her. After a moment he went on, 'But I was only twenty-one, and the blood runs hot then. It was never a very satisfactory fantasy, too much like taking pleasure in the beating of a child. Now you are a much more worthy opponent. Conquering that proud spirit will be a victory to savour, a prize worth the taking.'

His smile told her that he meant every word of it. With suddenly dry lips she said as lightly as she could, 'How would you like to begin? Would it pander to your delusions of omnipotence if I tremble at your approach?'

The smile widened. 'Why, no, for what pleasure would it give me to break you if you were already broken?'

Very gravely she met the fierce anticipation in his regard. 'What do you plan to do to produce that result? Whip me?'

'No, I shall not beat you, although most of my countrymen would think me crazy for not teaching you that sort of lesson. I have no stomach for torture.' He used his thumb to pull her softly swollen bottom lip down and leaned over so that his breath came hot and steady on the sensitive skin. 'I do not intend to tell you what I plan to do with you, Amber. That way you will not be able to build defences. Now, come and see your prison.'

A chill of fear slithered the length of her backbone, but she ignored it, allowing her hand to lie limply in his as he led her through the scented throbbing air down a path beneath the trees to the house.

'A very beautiful prison,' she said when she saw it.

'I can claim no credit for its beauty. It was built by an

American who wanted nothing to spoil the natural ambience of the place. That is why he chose stained timber. From the sea it is almost impossible to see the house.'

Amber nodded, looking about her with a pleasure made keener, sharper, by apprehension. 'I like the way native trees and shrubs are used in the garden,' she observed. 'They tie the house into its surroundings.'

'Clearly he hired an excellent landscape gardener,' Alex returned without interest as he inserted a key into the lock.

Inside the house was clean and sparse and cool, with the same stained wood contrasting with walls in a pale tint of blue. Curtains of a deeper hue framed magnificent views over the bay to another island about three miles away, and beyond it the mainland, here steep and inhospitable, blue-green with the heavy, mysterious jungle which New Zealanders called the bush.

'There is no way to get there,' Alex said evenly, following the line of her gaze. 'Unless you swim.'

Her shoulders hunched in a stiff little shrug before she turned away from the tantalising glimpse of freedom. 'I would drown before I made it, and I have people who depend on me.'

He bared his teeth. 'But you will forget about them while you are here. I do not want to hear their names, or see that faraway look in your eyes which means that you are thinking of them.'

His fingers slid into the soft warm curls at the back of her neck, tugging with a gentle insistence so that she was forced to obey, to tilt her head backwards and expose the creamy length of her throat to him in the classic gesture of submission.

His mouth was heated and slightly cruel, but although she could feel the sharpness of his teeth as they grazed the delicate skin, he did not hurt her. After a moment he muttered, 'While you are here you belong to me, mind, body, and soul. There will be no room for anyone else in your thoughts. Do you understand me?'

'Yes,' she said, and when he did not release her she said it again, feeling the points of tension along her bared throat coalesce almost into pain.

He pressed an open-mouthed kiss against the heavily beating pulse at the base and let her go, watching from beneath sculptured lids as she took a step backwards. 'Come and see the rest of the house,' he commanded after a tense moment.

It too was spartan in its simplicity; just a huge bedroom with a square wooden bed covered by a Greek embroidery in wool, green and blue and gold, with doors leading off it presumably to a dressing-room and bathroom, and on the other side of the sitting-room a kitchen with a table beside another window overlooking that glorious view. From every room big sliding glass doors opened out on to a wide deck along the entire front of the house. It was partly shaded by a pergola draped with a vine and there were loungers and chairs enough to idle away any number of summer days.

'A cup of coffee, I think,' Alex suggested matter-of-factly. 'You look hot. Do you wish to shower?'

Amber was suddenly, shamingly, conscious of the fact that she probably smelt of horse and sweat, but she hesitated just long enough for him to give her an unkind smile and taunt, 'I think I can manage to restrain my animal instincts until tonight. I'll make some coffee—or would you prefer a cold drink?'

'Coffee,' she said quickly because it would take him longer, and walked back into that huge shadowed bedroom.

After a moment she tried one of the doors in the wall, relaxing as she walked into a small wood-panelled bathroom. A towelling robe hung on a hook; she took it down, turned on the shower and dropped her clothes on to the floor.

Examining her emotions beneath the cool mist of the shower, she wondered why she was not more afraid. She shivered a little, remembering the tales Alex's father had enjoyed telling of the long, ferocious resistance against their enemies made by the Greeks over centuries of oppression. History had hardened them, made them savage in the pursuit of vengeance, strengthened their souls with the iron of bitterness.

Beneath the sophisticated exterior of the man who headed the billion-dollar Stephanides Corporation were the reactions and attitudes of the outlaws who had roamed the barren mountains of Greece, swooping down like starving wolves on those who robbed them of their inheritance. Harsh strength and ruthlessness had been bred in Alex's bones; it was, in part, what had made him the head of one of the biggest business empires in the world.

Yes, deep in the hidden parts of her mind she had always expected him to find her, and make her pay for the insult she had flung in his proud face. And that knowledge had strengthened her. Humiliation was in the mind; if she didn't allow it, he could not shame her. The only thing he could do to her was rape her, and she was prepared for that too.

The important thing was to hide the fact that he had a son. She would not allow him to take Nick and bring him up to accept that barbaric code of behaviour in which women were prey or dolls. Nick would respect women, and if she had her way his marriage would be a meeting of minds based on true liking and appreciation as well as the incandescent sexual rapture she had known in his father's arms.

She pushed those memories to the back of her brain, reminding herself grimly just how little that maddened passion had meant to him. For a few short weeks she had been rapturously happy, blinded by the fierce sweetness of their lovemaking into thinking they would be able to build a marriage which would make a mockery of the divorce statistics and the gossip columnists. And then his stepmother had told her casually and maliciously of the mistress he kept at a convenient house in Iraklion, not very far away.

Amber hadn't believed her. How could she? She had been seventeen, with a head stuffed full of romantic dreams. It hadn't even occurred to her that Alex's expertise in bed came from a vast experience. So she had taxed him with it, and he had been very angry with his stepmother, but he had not denied it.

Amber's mouth twisted in an unconscious grimace. She could still feel the bitter taste of betrayal on her tongue. She had wept, and demanded to go back home, and threatened him with the loss of her love, of her body, and he had been gentle and implacable and reasonable, taking her in spite of her resistance and her bitter protests, shaming her because he had taught her too well to respond to him with all the mindless intensity of her passionate nature. Angry and disillusioned though she was, her body still submitted to the merciless demand of his.

But she had not submitted, and after a few weeks her continued bitter objections had angered him. Angry, the grey eyes stormy in his autocratic face, he had given up his pose of calm reason and told her that if she was not prepared to fulfil her duties as his wife he would go to a woman who would. And he would not touch her again until she came to him and asked. He had spoken cruelly, his mouth thin and contemptuous as though he had expected her to surrender almost immediately to the fires he had kindled in her.

It was that, more than his unfaithfulness, which had opened her eyes to his low opinion of her sex. He really thought that she was so weak, so much a prey to her new-found needs that she would be prepared to share him. And he made it quite clear he considered that his occasional use of her body and the careless bestowal of clothes and jewellery and luxurious living should be enough to satisfy her.

So, wounded but fighting with the only weapons she possessed, she had determined never to give in. For a whole month they had shared the big bed, and although she had ached with longing, been burned by its intolerable intensity, she had held herself aloof.

And through it all, Alex had continued to visit his mistress.

That humiliation burned deep, but she might have learned to accept the situation simply because she had nowhere to go, no possibility of supporting herself. Her mother had been dead for a year and she knew that she would get no help from her father. But one day, less than a month later, her stepmother pointed Gabrielle Patoux out in the street. Amber saw an exquisite Frenchwoman with more allure in the enticing curve of her lips than Amber had in all her youthful body, but it was not the woman's looks that whitened Amber's face. It was the fact that she was pregnant.

From that moment the anger and humiliation which had fired her resistance turned to corrosive hatred. She had said nothing, turning all her thoughts to plan her escape from a situation which had become unbearable.

It had taken more acting ability than she knew she possessed not to betray the decision she had made, but she had done it, bleakly glad that Alex was still punishing her by not touching her. A few weeks later he had taken her with him to London where they had spent the night in her father's house. The next morning Alex had left to go to New York and twenty-four hours later there had been a photograph of him in a newspaper, at a nightclub, smiling with his predatory charm into the enraptured face of a woman notorious for the number and wealth of her lovers.

An outraged, heartbroken Amber had stolen away to

the unknown cousin on the other side of the world, not realising then that on that very last night together at her father's house when Alex had taken her with automatic passion in the middle of the night, he had made her pregnant.

It had not taken her long to learn how to be happy again. After the painful hours of labour when Nick was put in her arms she had vowed her life to his welfare, and in Matt's undemanding affection and the pleasant life she loved she had found happiness; it was strange to realise now that there had always been an element of foreboding in her contentment. Some part of her had known that Alex would see to it that she paid for it.

Well, it had been worth it, she thought as she turned the water off. Nine years of peace were more than a lot of people got. She would be free after she allowed Alex to indulge his taste for vengeance. And if the thought did not repel her as it should have, she thrust the knowledge back into her subconscious, refusing to face it.

The smell of coffee tantalised her nostrils as she came into the kitchen. Nine years since she had had Greek coffee, she thought wryly. It had been one of her bugbears, the thick syrupy stuff, far too strong for her, but in those days she had drunk little more than orange juice. Now she had become accustomed to coffee, and tea and the other stimulants.

Alex was standing at the window, watching a yacht tack to and fro in the bay beyond. He turned his sleek black head as she came through the door, his dark eyes moving with open appreciation from her damp hair to the tanned slender length of her legs exposed beneath the hem of the robe.

Colour rose from her throat, but she said conversationally, 'I couldn't find anything else to wear and my clothes smell very strongly of horse!'

He lifted his brows at that. 'Fastidious as ever! There is a door in the panelling on the other side of the bedroom which leads to a dressing-room. I had the clothes you will wear put there.'

She nodded and began to turn, but he said, 'Drink your coffee. I like the look of those long English legs beneath my robe.'

'Speaking of long legs,' she said with aloof composure, 'how is Gabrielle?'

The wide shoulders moved in a shrug and there was no alteration in his expression. 'Well.'

'And the baby? Was it a girl or a boy?'

'It died,' he returned icily. 'It was a boy.'

Amber bit her lip, then said with quiet sincerity, 'I'm sorry, that must have been a blow to you both.'

'I cannot believe you mean that.'

The coffee was more pleasant than she remembered, but she still discerned a hint of the flavour of wet tee-shirts which used to upset her. 'I do,' she said, wishing heartily that she hadn't succumbed to the ignoble desire to hurt. 'Losing a child must be about the worst thing that can happen to a woman.'

Alex's mouth hardened to a thin line. As his lashes came down to hood his eyes he said sarcastically, 'Forgive me if I find it a little difficult to reconcile my memory of your professed hatred of my mistress with this apparent concern for her well-being.'

Uneasiness, the feeling that somehow she had made a most damaging admission, hurried her into speech. 'I spent so much time hating her that it seems the least I can do is to wish her well now.'

'And when,' he asked in a soft deadly voice, 'did you begin to lose this hatred of her?'

She sipped her coffee, determined not to be intimidated. 'When I accepted the fact that she was as much a victim as I was,' she told him serenely.

For a second she read astounded shock in the arrogant features until he smiled and said with cool menace, 'Were you my victim, Amber? How melodramatic! I had no idea you lived such a vigorous fantasy life.'

'Not entirely. A victim of my own romantic dreams.'
She shrugged, her expression derisive as she recalled the
schoolgirl she had been. 'I thought that love was the sum
of woman's whole existence. I'm afraid I was very naïve.
Astoundingly so, when you think of it, because most of
the other girls at school were far more sensible. I didn't
even know then that my father went in for lechery on a
big scale. My mother kept up a pretty good front. If I had
known, perhaps I wouldn't have tried so hard to win his
love. That's one of the reasons I married you, you know.
It was the first thing I'd been able to do for him in my
life, the only thing I'd ever done that pleased him. Unfortunately no one bothered to explain the rules to me.'

Alex said calmly, 'Are you trying to make me sorry for
you, Amber?'

'God, no! I wallowed in enough self-pity to keep me
going for the rest of my life.' She directed a mocking
smile at the strong impassive line of his profile, inviting
him to share the joke. 'You see, as well as hoping to
please my father, I tumbled headlong into what I thought
was love.'

'But you soon discovered that it was not so. Within a
month of the last time we made love together you were in
your cousin's bed.' His voice was casual as though they
were discussing the weather; she could read nothing in
his shuttered face.

Her lips parted, then clamped shut. To hide the fact
that she was at a loss she drank some more coffee. That
night in London he and her father had sat up late, talking
and drinking, and when at last he came to bed Alex had
fallen asleep almost immediately. It had been almost a
month after he had begun his war of attrition, refusing to
touch her, cynically using her youthful adoration and the
needs of her awakened body as weapons against her.

Stiff and antagonistic on her side of the big double bed,
Amber had finally drifted off, satisfied that this would be

the last time she shared a bed with him. A few hours later she had been woken by caresses, tender and expert, and in mindless submission had played her part in the age-old game of passion, silent in the darkened room.

In the morning he had made no reference to it, treating her once more with the cool withdrawal which so hurt her. Something in his eyes told her that he did not know that he had claimed her with such gentle, erotic unconsciousness, that he must have been only half-awake, and she had wondered if he would ever recall it.'

Now she knew. He did not, and it was thanks to that that she was able to hide the fact of his paternity from him.

'So it was not much of a love,' he said evenly after a few moments, still watching with an intentness she found nerve-racking. 'Perhaps you are not a woman who loves, Amber. Perhaps any man can have the gasping little words that come from deep in your throat, the wild throes of ecstasy when you behave like a bacchante, untamed and savage and a little bit frightening; is it easy for any man to rouse you, so that you welcome him into the smooth delight of your body with the same joyous paganism you offered me?'

The evocative words brought heat burning slowly through her loins and breasts. She clenched her hand to keep it from trembling and then relaxed it, because the movement was a betrayal. But he had seen it, and he laughed deep in his throat and came on silent panther strides to where she sat at the table and slid his thumb across her mouth, using it to force the lower lip down.

She stiffened, but her eyes met the smoky fire of his fearlessly until his questing hand slid slowly the length of her throat and tightened around its slenderness.

'A hundred years ago no one would have been surprised if I strangled you,' he said, each silky word heavy with menace. 'It would have been considered a normal, even honourable way to behave to an adulteress.

Even today most men would understand the strength of my need to wipe out your treachery in some cataclysmic action.'

His fingers tightened, but through the drumming in her ears she returned, 'The days when women are treated as objects is over in the Western world, Alex. I don't belong to you—I never have. My body isn't a possession you can guard inviolate in a vault. And if you strangle me in New Zealand all that power you wield so ruthlessly will not keep you out of prison.'

He smiled sardonically and released her, saying as he straightened, 'No doubt. Fortunately for us both, I have no desire to kill you, merely to toy with you for a little while. But not now. I have work to do.'

And he strode off through the kitchen, whistling as though he had not just insulted her.

Amber stared after him, the skin over her high cheekbones prickling with anger, then got to her feet and washed the cups and saucers before making her way back to the bedroom. Carefully averting her eyes from the big bed, she found the door which led into her dressing-room, and sure enough, there in a wall of cupboards and drawers were the clothes he had ordered for her.

They were exquisitely made in materials of the best quality, satins and silks and pure, fine cotton, but after she had tried on a few she stormed back into the bathroom and washed out the cotton shirt and shorts, the bra and pants she had been wearing. The clothes he had chosen had been carefully and deliberately ordered to reinforce his attitude of contempt towards her. Tight, low-cut, flagrantly designed to emphasise the sexual attributes of the woman who wore them, they were another insult, and they were not going to touch her skin.

Shaking with anger, she marched through the kitchen to the back door, looking for the clothes line. A path led through the thick shrubbery to a rotary hoist in the middle of a small patch of wiry, uncut grass. She hung the clothes there, fixing each plastic peg with a vicious little twist, then paced back into the house.

The sound of Alex's voice made her jump; she stopped, and stared around, realising after a moment that the house was built on a steep slope and below the main storey was another room, presumably an office. Well, of course, the wretched Stephanides Corporation could not continue to rake in billions of dollars without the almost constant surveillance of the despot who ran it!

Still fuming, she turned down a path which led to the beach, dragging the wretched robe free of the bushes which caught at the hem. The sand was a pale beige-pink, hot beneath her feet, the little beach sheltered from the sea by a reef of rocks which gave it almost complete privacy, for as they were just below the level of the water they made passage into the bay impossible for anything bigger than a dinghy. About a hundred yards offshore a raft was moored; Amber flung off the robe and ran into the water, swimming with a strong crawl out to it.

Once on it she sat cross-legged, staring sightlessly out to sea, her straight back eloquent of her anger. She knew that she was safe for quite some time; Alex spent long hours on his business. He was not a workaholic like her father, but the ramifications of such a far-flung empire required almost constant supervision. She recalled an article she had read about the Corporation, a glowing, eulogistic summary of successes and coups which had detailed its structure while making it quite plain that Alex was at once the overseeing intelligence and the power. In positions of responsibility were the cousins and the two brothers who helped him run it, but Alex was the boss.

The sun streamed down on her shoulders and face, its strength making her skin tingle. Reluctantly she dived neatly off the raft. It was folly to go out into the northern summer without protection. But she dawdled, playing a little while in the water, deliberately emptying her mind of what the night would bring, before striking back for the shore. As she waded up towards the beach she pushed her soaking curls back and lifted her small face to the sky, standing with closed eyes while the sun glared red through her eyelids.

The touch on her cheek elicited a startled little cry from her as her lashes flew upwards and she realised that she had grossly overestimated the time it would take Alex to finish his business.

He was watching the water stream from her smooth golden body with a tight smile, a muscle pulling beside the controlled line of his mouth. Instantly her skin contracted and she stepped back, loathing the insolent slide of his eyes over her.

His jaw hardened; through his teeth he said, 'Perhaps the first lesson you must learn is that you do not flinch away from my touch.'

And even as she realised that the quick involuntary movement had roused the hunter his hands went to her breast and between her thighs.

That was when she realised that she hadn't really believed that he would go ahead with it. Even as she gasped in outrage the knowledge burned into her brain that once again she had underestimated this Greek husband of hers, attributing to him a code of behaviour which she thought civilised but he would consider effete and weak.

She stiffened but made no protest, merely closing her eyes to hide the cold desire in his face. The long fingers moved and were withdrawn.

'No,' he said huskily, 'I do not wish to hurt you.'

Amber opened her eyes. 'I thought that was the idea.'

His mouth compressed. 'Give me credit for a little subtlety,' he said obliquely as he stepped back.

As a reply it was not at all reassuring. She gave him credit for a great deal of subtlety, and she felt the first stirrings of real fear, quickly masking her eyes so that he could not discern her apprehension.

He looked around him with keen appreciation, saying, 'This reminds me a little of home. Is the water as warm?'

When she had wrapped the robe around herself she replied, 'No, and it doesn't get as hot here as it does in Crete, but we can have lovely summers, long and dry and hot. Normally the countryside is a lot drier at this time of the year, but we had a warm, wet spring and the grass is still growing.'

He nodded. 'I noticed.' His eyes ran over her once more and he touched the back of his hand to her cheek. 'You are a little burned, I think. In the bathroom there is a sunblock which you will use before you come out into the sun again. Wait in the shade for me while I swim.'

Amber bristled at the calm command, but after a moment during which he watched her with an enigmatic little smile as though challenging her to object, she sat down on the cool sand beneath a wide overhanging branch of one of the big pohutukawas and hugged her knees, trying not to look as he stripped down to nothing and walked across the sand with the tight controlled grace of a predator.

The nine years that had elapsed had thickened that lean body slightly; at twenty-one he had not been as muscular as he was now, but the lithe understated stride of those long legs was the same, and the total, unabashed enjoyment of his strength and health which saw nothing shameful in nudity.

In purely physical terms he was sinfully attractive and potently, powerfully desirable in a way which had little to do with his outstanding natural attributes. The classical perfection of his features delighted the eye, yet he could have been ugly and women would still have wanted him. Money? No, it was his pride and that rock-bottom self-assurance, and something else, an intangible quality which compelled the interest and attention of every woman.

Amber watched his dark arms cleave through the water with mutiny brooding in the back of her eyes. As well as promising the forbidden delights of the damned, he possessed a strong protective instinct that appealed to all that was weak and feminine. He could smile and the woman who was the object of his interest felt at once cared for and the most desirable woman in the world.

And the obverse of that, she told herself sternly, fighting a bewildering surge of emotion, is that he considers women to be useful for three things only—to provide children, to keep the house comfortable, and to give him physical release.

It had not been enough for her at seventeen; it was ridiculous to allow herself to be touched by his sexuality now.

Think of poor Gabrielle, who had borne his child and lost it, who still lived only on the fringes of his life. Did she love him? Had there been other children for her? Strange, she had hated Gabrielle, and yet now all she could feel for her was a vast pity. Arrogant, stubborn, dominating *Greek*, she thought wearily, and when he came up out of the water like Poseidon rising above the Aegean she looked at him with resentment sparking the warm golden glow of her eyes into a glittering glory.

He smiled and said softly, 'That is how I like to see you, with your defiant spirit shining out through your eyes.'

'That,' she returned without visible emotion, 'is because you're a bully. You enjoy subduing resistance.'

The broad, wet shoulders moved in a shrug. He bent to pick up his towel and Amber turned her head away, appalled at the shaft of lust which arrowed through her at the flexion of muscles beneath warm brown skin. Her fingertips tingled at remembered sensations, silk over steel, the erotic patterns of hair which accented the forceful masculinity of his torso, and his particular scent, clean and slightly salty with a hint of musk which became stronger as he was aroused. The old heated languor seeped like a tide of honey through her body and she was both shamed and angered by her involuntary response to the easy physical lure of the man.

The towel which had been blotting the rivulets of sea water from his face stilled; he tossed it around his shoulders and came across to where she sat huddled away from him. He was smiling unpleasantly as he bent a little to catch her by the elbows and pull her to her feet.

She averted her face, helpless to hide to her reaction. Deep in his throat he laughed, and a cool firm hand curved around her chin, forcing her face up to meet the cloudy turbulence of his gaze.

'A bully?' he jeered. 'Oh no, my sweet wanton, I shall not bully you into my bed. I am not so crass. When we make love it will be because you want me.'

'You can't help it, I suppose,' Amber retorted as calmly as she could. 'Being an egotist, I mean. From all accounts your mother ruined you, and your father was another who thought that a woman's sole function was to put her head beneath her husband's heel. But I'd like to know what gave you the idea that you can whistle me into your bed as though I'm totally without will or strength of mind!'

His taunting eyes swept indolently across her angry face. 'At least you do not pretend that you are immune to me. Sensible of you, because while this little pulse throbs in your throat,' his mouth came to rest on the small traitor, and he spoke against her skin, 'and while your eyes widen each time they rest on me, I know that you want me. As for the strength of will,' he lifted his head and smiled into her face, hard, confident, insulting, 'that, heart of my delight, is what is going to make the next few days so interesting.'

Amber hid a sudden unnerving terror with scorn. 'Such conceit!'

'Is that a challenge?'

His eyes were narrowed, secretive, as though he knew something she didn't. He was clever, he had an armoury of tricks and ploys, he was an exceptionally good actor; it helped in the all-out confrontations, the subtle, lethal battles which were his daily fare in the world he inhabited, but she refused to be intimidated.

Haughtily she moved away, surprised when he let her go. Her feet sank into the cool soft sand beneath the tree as she said evenly, 'No, you're the one who likes challenges, not me. All I want is a quiet life.'

There had been irony in his smile, but at her words it broadened, and for a moment the cynical depths of his eyes cleared and she saw real amusement there. It was strangely warming and she had to bite her lip to prevent an answering gleam. It was too easy to forget that he was far too experienced not to know exactly how he was affecting her with his sudden shifts of mood. But if she had read him right he was not going to force her. His lust for vengeance would only be satisfied if he lured her to him. What had he said? *I will hear you beg*, he had promised.

A chilly premonition tightened her skin into gooseflesh. She fought it, lifting her head with unconscious arrogance. No longer the child who had thought she loved him, she was now an adult, a woman. She had suffered, she had borne a child and known that it depended entirely on her. She had discovered in herself the strength to refuse him that surrender.

She had to, because she was far from immune to his dark sexuality. Chemistry, she reminded herself sternly, that's all. Scent, or something. The pull of eager man for available woman. A primeval urge as basic as the need to eat and sleep.

Something of her thoughts must have showed in her

face, for Alex frowned and bent his head and bit her lip, not too gently, waiting as she opened her mouth on a breath of astonishment before storming into the sweet depths. The sharp, unexpected assault struck her rigid and he pulled her into the long, lean length of his body, using his strength to throw her off balance.

Amber was suffocated by him, seared by a flame of sensation which ran from the base of her spine to her thighs, and thence to every nerve-end through her body.

His mouth gentled, savoured hers, moved from the stifling invasive barbarity of that first kiss to a seducing heated eroticism which made her tremble. It was nine years since a man had kissed her. Nine long years, and though she thought she had been happy in them they now seemed empty and barren of all that made life worthwhile.

Surprised, she gave a little wordless murmur and he gathered her closer, imprisoning her against his hardening body until she panicked and began to struggle. Even then he did not release her straight away but said softly and with mocking satisfaction, 'You see, it is simple for me to make you forget the years when you have graced another man's bed. I don't think I will have to wait very long for you, Amber.'

She searched for an answer, but none came. Instead she stepped away, firming lips which felt an urge to tremble, and began to walk back up the beach, intolerably shaken by the weakness of her body.

Alex caught her up and tucked her hand into his arm. She remembered this physicality, his pleasure in touch, as Greek as his appetite for life and his passionate delight in it, and the fierce hunger for vengeance. Alarmed, she hesitated, but he paid no attention, and began to tell her of a coup he had just pulled off.

Nine years ago he would not have bothered and she would not have been interested, but she was now. Tentatively at first, because any relaxation of her guard was fraught with danger, she began to ask questions. He answered them, explaining the reasons for his actions, and she found him fascinating; too attractive when his eyes gleamed with amusement and enjoyment and an oddly endearing satisfaction as he spoke.

She almost forgot that he was naked and she as near to it as made no difference as she listened with absorption, because what he was telling her was enthralling, a kind of romance complete with villains and white knights and court jesters, and at its conclusion she laughed irrepressibly, her long eyes alight with humour.

Lazy amusement quirked his lips. 'More interesting than sheep and cattle?' he taunted, disconcertingly.

She bit her lip but said, 'Not in the least. Just different.'

'You never used to lie. It was what I liked about you, that stark, almost brutal honesty.'

She said wearily, 'A child's honesty. I hadn't realised that childish responses only applied to childish situations. You taught me otherwise.'

Alex opened the door into the house and waited while she went through. 'It was just as well, for it was time for you to grow up.'

'True.'

'But not, perhaps, so brutally.'

Amber swung around to stare at him in astonishment. He looked amused at her obvious surprise and a little patronising, and she felt her hackles lift. Turning away from him, she said unemotionally, 'Oh, I don't know. It could have been even more brutal. Imagine if I'd really been in love with you, instead of suffering from my first schoolgirl crush.'

'Imagine,' he agreed carelessly. His hand on her shoulder was not unexpected, but he said merely, 'There is a bathroom off your dressing-room. Use it. This time I want you to use the clothes I have bought for you.'

'I'm not wearing them.'

'Indeed? Then you can go naked.' He let her go and continued in a voice from which every scrap of expression had gone, 'The decision is yours, my dear. But if you do not put on the clothes I have bought for you then they will all be burned, the ones you were wearing as well. While you are with me you will wear only clothes of my providing. I do not care a bit whether you like them or not, they were not bought to please you.'

Her whole being rose in protest, but she recognised the implacable intention behind the words. To be forced into nudity would be unbearable, and he would do it. Without a word she left him and walked through the dressing-room and beyond it into the bathroom.

She had used his before, and expected hers to be the same, so the first sight of it stopped her just inside the door. From behind she heard his soft taunting laughter, and then she slammed the door.

The American millionaire had indulged all his sybaritic fantasies in the bathroom; it was completely over the top, decorated in a kind of flamboyant yet naïve splendour which owed something to the lure of the Orient and a lot to Hollywood's influence. If Amber had not been so angry and apprehensive she would have loved it, from the crystal chandelier in the ceiling to the wide marble bath and the mosaic tiles on the floor and walls, tiny cubes of gold and green and blue in a pattern which reminded her of her one visit to the Alhambra in Spain, that monument to the sophistication and worldliness of the Moors who had built it.

Water jetted from gold dolphins, and in a wall devoted to cupboards there were towels and lotions and perfumes, body oils spiked with the faint musk and lush florals of the East, a complete set of the cosmetics she still wore.

Amber stared at them, biting her lip until the pain made her release it with a gasp, hating the cynical lack of respect which underlined the charming conceit. Alex meant her to understand how powerless she was if he chose to make the fantasy a reality; this was a room for a slave girl, a concubine, whose only aim in life was to please her master.

As she took off the wrap her expression hardened into severity. Alex's wounded pride needed her surrender, even if it was only to the common coin of physical desire, but he was too skilled in sexual combat to rape her. The meaning of this charade wasn't hard to understand. He was determined that she should learn the limits of her powerlessness, and threading through the subtle aggression would be his ruthless use of the attraction that still beat like a dark wild force between them.

The sensible thing to do would be to give in, get it over and done with so that they could both go back to their lives. Deny him the surrender he needed with a calm impersonal acceptance of him as a lover. Behave like the bought mistress he intended her to be.

But the liquid feeling in her loins made her almost run across the room and step down into that opulent bath. Once in it she soaped herself with brisk impersonality, but slowly her hands slowed, and she bent forward, hiding her face behind the clustering curls as she pondered. Would surrender be so drastic?

She had no need to consider it. Her breath shuddered through her body as she stiffened. Yes, it would. At the very least Alex could make her pregnant again. Even as her features softened she made a sound of fear. That would be asking for trouble; he wouldn't let a child of theirs stay with her.

But the real reason for her rejection of the idea was that she knew now that calm impersonality was beyond her; she could not treat a liaison with him as just a distasteful interruption in her normal life. She was not built that way.

So, she decided as she stood up with a quick decisive movement, she was just going to have to summon up all the willpower she possessed and keep him at bay.

As a defence it was riddled with holes. Alex had monumental patience but a quick temper. And he was accustomed to easy conquests. If she infuriated him past control he might react with violence.

A shiver of apprehension chilled her skin. She had never seen him lose control; he used his temper to intimdate, but she didn't think he ever allowed it to go beyond his ability to restrain it. And she doubted if he would allow a woman to force his temper past the guards he set on it. Deep inside, her smiling, sexy husband had little but contempt for women. He might deny it even to himself, but he thought them inferior beings.

So it was highly unlikely that he would become angry enough to rape her, because he would see such a loss of control to mean that she had some power over him.

CHAPTER THREE

SATISFIED, Amber smiled and drew the towel across her breasts, freeing them from the filmy veil of bubbles. A tiny traitor in her brain wondered if Alex would find her much different from the seventeen-year-old who had graced his bed for such a short time nine years ago, and she was appalled to realise that that same treacherous part of her mind was being quietly congratulatory because she had the sort of skin which coped very adequately with pregnancy. Her breasts were a little fuller, her waist not quite so narrow, but the few stretch marks she had discovered were by now almost invisible on the flat tautness of her stomach.

Colour burned across her cheeks. With a defiant little gesture she ran her hands down the sleek wet length of her body to wipe away the soap.

'What were you thinking?'

She whirled, lost her balance on the slippery marble and landed flat in the water with a tremendous splash which took her breath away entirely. Choking, she began to cough, tears starting to her eyes as she flailed around.

When she could see again Alex was crouched by the bath, concern darkening his eyes. He had grabbed her by the upper arms and seated her and was now holding her upright.

'Are you all right?' he demanded, and when she didn't answer his hands tightened and he used his incredible strength to haul her up out of the scented water and set her on her feet, still gripping her. 'Tell me, did you hurt yourself?'

'No, only my composure, damn you!' She gave a final cough and wiped a layer of froth from her mouth before

49

continuing furiously, 'How dare you startle me like that. Get the hell out of here!'

He laughed, sudden amusement wiping the rare solicitude from his expression as swiftly as if it had never been there. 'You look like a child, soft and pink and sweetly scented, with bubbles all over you. And a child's tantrum making your eyes snap sparks at me.'

The hard impersonal grasp eased; now, as the humour faded to be replaced by something much more sinister, his hands slipped across her wet skin from her arms to her shoulders and then up to the delicate strong column of her throat and his possessive glance slid over her body. 'No, not like a child,' he said thickly, and watched as colour flooded the satin gilt of her skin and her fists clenched impotently at her sides.

'Get out,' she whispered harshly. 'Leave me alone!'

He snared her eyes in the crystalline depths of his. 'No. I intend to look at you as often as I wish. That is why you are here, remember? So that I may sate myself with you past the point of desire. When I can look at this beautiful body without feeling anything more than appreciation for a living work of art, then you can go back to your lover. If he still wants you.'

Foolishly Amber averred, 'Nothing, *nothing* you can do will make any difference to the way Matt feels about me!'

His black brows lifted. With a smile glittering with malice he said, 'But what a lukewarm affair it must be, my Amber! If you think to convince him that you came unwillingly, remember that the child's mother saw you leave with me, without protest. Not even the most devoted of lovers would forgive a slight like that! But perhaps he would rather you made a whore of yourself than suffer bankruptcy and a life of poverty and degradation.'

She retorted savagely, 'If he does, is that any worse than blackmail?' and he dropped his hands as if she had at last stung him, answering in stony disdain, 'Perhaps not. Now, get dressed. You can prepare dinner. I have a few more calls to make.'

More than anything she longed to order him out of the room again, but after one fulminating glare at his implacable face she knew better than to try it. So she turned her back and snatched a towel, dragging it over her body with swift, angry movements, and when she looked up he had gone as silently as he came.

It was difficult to chase from her brain the memory of the way he had looked at her, the moments when an honest sensual appreciation had warmed his eyes, the moments before he had remembered that humiliation was the name of his game. That candid and enthusiastic appraisal of her nakedness had the power to make her realise that she was a desirable woman, one who had delighted in the pleasures of the flesh until betrayal had turned them bitter.

She kept the recollection at bay while she searched through the wardrobe and drawers in the dressing-room, finally settling on a pair of shorts cut tight and high in the leg, and a tube top, skimpy but not unbearably so. Refusing to even look at herself in the mirrors with which the room was plentifully supplied, she walked through to the kitchen.

Another search, through the refrigerator this time, revealed aubergine and peppers and beans, enough to make a ratatouille; she prepared the vegetables and put them on to stew, decided to have eggs with it, and rock melons with passion fruit as a pudding. For the first course she made soup with yoghurt and cucumbers, putting it back in the fridge to chill.

Then she went into the sitting-room and sat down on the sofa in front of the wide window and watched with a set face as the day moved graciously towards dusk. Tension thrummed through her body, and she breathed deeply and calmly, trying to calm herself down.

After all, although his lovemaking would be a humiliation, Alex could no longer hurt her. She had only to resist the weakness bred deep in her bones and eventually he must tire of his vengeful game. It would not surprise her if that was his intention; to seduce her until she was eager for him and then send her back with his contemptuous rejection shattering her pride. He had dismissed the idea before, but there had been pleasure of a sort in his deep voice as he told her of it.

Or perhaps he hoped that by keeping her here he would break up what he considered to be her affair with Matt. According to the code he lived by, the code his fierce father had drummed into him, any woman who slept with another man was a whore, and would be treated as such. He simply would not understand any other way of behaving.

Whatever his plans, she was immune as long as he didn't learn that he had a son. But that, she consoled herself, was unlikely. He must have known about Nick for some time, possibly even seen a photograph of him, and obviously it hadn't occurred to him to be suspicious.

Mildly comforted by this thought, she watched a speedboat tear across the bay, in its hurry narrowly missing a small sailing dinghy.

The sun beat on to the terrace outside, setting fire to geraniums and hibiscus, the only two plants vigorous enough to grow without care. Amber sat still, her long legs curled up beneath her, bright head drooping. She had kept up a brave front ever since the trauma of Alex's arrival, but beneath all the steadfast courage lurked fear, simple and stark and definite. He had given her his word that if she stayed with him he would not use his immense power to bankrupt Matt, but beyond that she did not trust him at all. Behind the worldly magnate was a man trained and encouraged to follow the primitive code of his ancestors. He wanted to break her, and she knew how frail and insubstantial her defences were.

Her face carefully composed to hide anxiety, she got to her feet and went into the kitchen to check the ratatouille.

A moment later she heard his footsteps on the narrow spiral staircase which came up from the lower storey. Tensely she waited. He came straight across to the kitchen, stopping in the doorway to comment with open appreciation, 'That smells good. What is it?'

After she told him he said smoothly, 'I am glad that you have not wasted the last nine years. You could not cook when you married me.'

Amber put the lid back on to the pan. 'I couldn't do much at all. Schoolgirls are pretty short on the practical side of life.'

'True.' The monosyllable was drawled out and when she looked at him he was smiling. 'I remember our wedding night.'

So did she—very vividly. She remembered her tension and fear of the unknown and how it was banished by his practised skills; she remembered her soaring, ecstatic introduction to the world of the senses, and her shaken, involuntary response. She had given herself, and he had taken everything and given her nothing in return.

'You were charmingly naïve,' he said, still smiling as he came closer. 'Sweet and unsophisticated and ignorant, but you learned how to please me very quickly. I enjoyed our wedding night, Amber, and the other nights that followed.'

'But not enough to stay faithful.' Her voice was cold; she felt stifled by his closeness but refused to back away.

Alex lifted his hand to thread a finger through a glowing tawny curl. Very softly, almost stealthily, the sensuous little movement was extended to the sensitive skin behind her ear. He was still smiling, his lashes hiding his eyes, but she could see the tightening of a small muscle beside his mouth and knew that he wanted her.

His voice was abstracted, as though he was thinking

aloud. 'Such a little prude! Surely you must have known that there had been women?'

Tiny beads of sweat sprang free of her skin. She took a deep breath, and said hoarsely, 'Of course I knew. Even at boarding school everyone knew of your amorous exploits. But knowing is one thing, experiencing it another. In my naïveté, my *unsophisticated ignorance*, I thought that a promise of faithfulness came with the marriage vows.'

That tormenting finger moved slowly to trace out the small spiral of her ear. She saw his chest lift suddenly, and he bent his head a little closer, his voice dropping to a deep, warm murmur. The scent of his masculinity, still as startlingly familiar as it had been the first time she had noticed it, curled through her as potently as a drug.

'But you knew that ours was a business alliance,' he said cruelly. 'It was obvious that although you found me attractive, you would not have considered me for a husband if it had not been for the pact made between your father and mine.'

Holding her breath against the pleasure which pierced her body, Amber realised wearily that he had seen through her as if she had been transparent. Yes, she had known that their marriage was a straight commercial transaction, but her longing to please her father had kept her silent. And in those weeks between their meeting and the engagement she had tumbled into love.

She could not say a word, and Alex finished with smooth malice, 'You knew. You were very unsophisticated, my Amber, but not, I think, stupid.'

'Oh, you're too kind. I was stupid—and wildly, romantically attracted to you. But you knew that, didn't you? You wanted me to fall in love with you. You set out to make it happen. I was seventeen, and you were an experienced, sophisticated twenty-one. I didn't have a chance. You banked on using my calf love to keep me sweetly, brainlessly devoted while you entertained yourself with your much more knowledgeable and exciting mistresses.'

Her voice wavered; to her horror she felt tears sting at the back of her eyes. She went on swiftly, 'If you'd told me beforehand how it was going to be, given me some choice in the matter so that I could have refused or accepted it—but you played me for a fool, you betrayed me. To you I was just a convenience.'

His hand dropped to her shoulder, gripped, and slid to the nape of her neck, tangling in the hair there. Harshly, his features rigid and autocratic, he said, 'You were my wife.'

'And therefore honoured above all other women.' The words dripped sarcasm. She stared unflinchingly into the cold grey depths of his eyes and said bitterly, 'Did you really think it would be enough to persuade me to put up with your deceit and betrayal? You have a monumental conceit, Alex! It wasn't enough. I felt just like all the other whores you bought. I couldn't live in an atmosphere of contempt, where women—all women—are considered playthings, toys to pass an idle hour, but not worthy of respect or understanding or liking. You were married to your business. Poor Gabrielle and I and the other women you used were very peripheral.'

He was furious. She could sense the frustrated rage emanating from him like a dark aura and she swallowed. Instantly the frozen fire of his gaze found the movement of the muscles in her slender throat. She felt the impact as if it were a blow. His mouth curved in a small meaningless smile, and fear shafted through her like a sword, the age-old primitive terror of weakness before strength, woman before barbaric man. A tiny sound escaped through her lips.

Slowly, with sinister purpose, his eyes moved until they fixed on her mouth in a strange intensity that called forth a blind response from her deepest being. Her lips burned; without thought she touched them with her tongue.

Instantly his eyes narrowed and he said in a voice that was heavy with satisfaction, 'And yet for all that, however despicable you find me, you want me. You cannot deny it, it is written in your face. That submissive lust is impossible to hide. Against every principle, every feminist instinct, you want what I can give you.'

Amber couldn't speak because she was transfixed by a desire so intense that if she had made any noise it would have been a cry of naked need. Through the window the setting sun streamed in a flood of rosy gold, creating an aureole around his dark hard face, caressing his hair with flame. A flame that was answered in his eyes, a searing mixture of passion and scorn irradiating the fierce arrogance of his features.

When she tried to twist away his fingers tightened in her hair to the point of pain, holding her face open to his inspection.

Smiling, although there was no humour in it, he said, 'I think you have all the instincts of a mistress, Amber. And by now you should have the experience, a wide knowledge of all the tricks that women use to pleasure a man, to make him lose himself in the sweet snare of their bodies for a moment out of time.'

She said, almost choking, 'No, I don't want you.'

'You are a liar.' The words came cruelly as he turned his head so that he could see her unconfined breasts beneath the thin knit material. They betrayed the stinging hunger in her as surely as any fifth columnist, and he laughed deep in his throat and pulled the strapless little top down and ran his hand over the tight, sensitive nubs in a caress as casual as it was humiliating before jerking the material back up and releasing her. In a voice suddenly smooth and devoid of emotion he said, 'Go and change while I pour drinks for us.'

So glad was she to escape that she had to stop herself

from running. Numbly, with nerves still taut and her body screaming for fulfilment, she forced one foot steadily after another back to the dressing-room.

Once there she stood helplessly, staring at herself in the two full-length mirrors. Her mouth was red and throbbing, her eyes languorous beneath heavy dazed lids. The skimpy top might not have been there, for all the good it did. Aching with shameful desire, she ripped it over her head and tore off the shorts before heading purposefully for her bathroom. There was no shower in there, but she splashed cold water on every part of her body, shivering slightly as she rubbed herself dry, flushed with mortification and anger.

She found a drawer full of sheer silk underwear, and eyed it with loathing, even going so far as to search the other drawers in case there was some less revealing underwear. Quite in vain, of course. In the end she chose a soft, transparent teddy, working on the assumption that the more layers she wore, however see-through they were, the better.

The dress she finally dragged over her head with almost total disregard for its fragility was a soft wisp of silk, almost the same colour as her skin. She chose it because it had a high neck, but a glance in the mirror when she was ready made her give a groan of chagrin. Like the tube top, it hid nothing; the material was so fine that it clung lovingly to every curve and contour of her body, as revealing, if not more, than anything slit to the navel could have been.

Defiantly she wriggled her feet into a pair of sandals the same colour, ran a comb through her hair, then with head held high went through into the sitting-room.

Alex stood up when she appeared, surveying her with coolly insolent appreciation, but he made no comment. He too had changed into another pair of well-tailored trousers and a silk shirt, Italian in style, the slight

flamboyance of its cut emphasising his darkly Mediterranean attraction.

Firmly repressing the leap in her blood, Amber said
the first thing that came to her lips. 'Champagne?'

'Of course. This is a celebration. We are reunited, you
and I. And I seem to remember that champagne was the
only alcohol you enjoyed.'

'I've overcome that,' she said drily. 'I'll just check
dinner.'

It was a retreat, and they both knew it. She stayed in
the kitchen for a few minutes, striving to overcome the
weakness in her loins and legs. Alex was not conceited;
he was too cynical for that, but he knew perfectly well
that he possessed a bone-deep magnetism which made
him almost irresistible to many women. Knew it, and
was unscrupulous enough to use it when he considered it
necessary.

Cold dismay iced through her veins as she wondered
for the first time whether she was going to be able to
escape from this situation without serious damage. She
stood for a moment biting her lip as she stared unseeing
down at the bowl of chilled soup. Then she straightened
her shoulders, added a drop of green food colouring to it
and stirred, before sliding it back into the refrigerator.

If she got hurt in this cat-and-mouse game it would be
more than worth it because it would save Nick from
Alex's influence, from developing the kind of heartless
attitude towards women which had betrayed and
humiliated her.

That thought gave her the courage to return to the
sitting-room, and to accept the glass he gave her, even to
smile a little as she sipped the delicious wine, enjoying in
spite of herself the break of bubbles over her tongue.

'How long have you owned this place?' she asked, as
politely as if they were meeting for the first time.

He knew what she was doing, of course; his eyes were
hooded when she lifted a calm face to his, but he followed

her lead readily enough. 'Only a few months. As soon as I discovered where you were I looked around for a place close enough to take you.' He smiled unpleasantly. 'I thought, you see, that I might have to kidnap you in real earnest. I did not then know that you were mercenary enough to surrender immediately at the threat of poverty. Would you sleep with anyone powerful enough to make the same threat?'

Amber paled at the vicious taunt but managed a shrug. 'I haven't slept with you.'

'You will,' he promised softly.

She drank a little more of the wine, then set the glass down. I'll have to keep a clear head, she said to herself. Aloud she murmured, 'I don't think anyone else should be punished for my actions. Matt has done you no wrong.'

Angry colour sprang into life along the hard line of his cheeks. 'Most men would think otherwise,' he pointed out too gently. 'Most men would object very strongly to a man who stole their wife.'

Amber sighed. 'That's the whole problem,' she said with no hope of being understood. 'He didn't steal me, because I am not an object to be disposed of. I made the decision to come here before I'd seen or met Matt. I came to New Zealand because he was the only relation I had in the world apart from my father, and I knew I wouldn't get any help from him! I didn't leave you for another man, I left you because I would not be treated as a thing of no account!'

Her voice had been rising as she remembered how much he had hurt her; abruptly she stopped, because to lose control would be to hand him an easy advantage, and walked across to the window, staring out at a sky the colour of crushed raspberries which glowed like a robe of rich satin in the west. Against it the bush-covered hills of the mainland were a stark cut-out, almost menacing. The sea gleamed with a reflection of the ruddy hues of the sunset, its surface a bowl of beaten metal in the hush of evening.

Alex watched her, his face impassive.

She made a hopeless little gesture and said, 'Why don't you let me go home, Alex? This desire for revenge is not worthy of you.'

Cynically he asked, 'In whose eyes? I can damn myself no further in yours, can I? No, you stay here until I have finished with you. For long years I have promised myself this interlude.' He paused, as though thinking, and when he spoke again the cynical arrogance had gone, to be replaced by a sombre inflection. 'You say that I did not know you, that I do not understand you. Very well then, show me what sort of person you are. And I in turn will show you myself.'

She turned eagerly, strangely so, and looked up into the handsome, implacable face. 'And will you—will you leave me alone?'

He laughed, very softly, and drew her into his arms, handling her with a confidence which revealed the depths of his assurance. 'Don't be foolish,' he whispered, brushing her startled eyes with the warm magic of his mouth. 'Why should I not enjoy what is still mine? You are my wife, Amber.'

'A ceremony and a piece of paper don't make a marriage,' she said stonily, torn by a disappointment so acute that she thought it ran like a stab of pain through her body.

'No, otherwise you would not have forgotten those vows we made.'

'I didn't forget them. You did. Or rather, you ignored them.'

She felt his mouth curve into a bitter smile. It smoothed a path over her hot cheek and down to the corner of her mouth, tasting, touching, the tip of his tongue savouring the smooth unpowdered skin. 'No make-up,' he murmured. 'Did you think it would dampen my ardour if you came out to me with a bare face? How foolish of you, Amber *mou*, if that is so. Your skin tastes of honey and spices, your mouth is as intoxicating as the champagne I can taste on it . . .'

The kiss was piercingly sweet, seducing her into opening her lips to him before she had time to summon her defences. She made a choked little sound in her throat and he gathered her against the quickening hardness of muscle and sinew that made up his lean body, the long arms pressing her intimately into him so that she felt his swift passionate awakening and took fire from it, her own slender length suddenly aflame with unconscious allure.

He muttered something in Greek, his voice strained and thick, then buried his mouth against her throat, bending her back to expose the silken length of it to his seeking kisses. Amber's breath dragged painfully through her lungs; she tightened her arms about his shoulders, almost frantic with excitement, all caution fled, all defences down, completely lost in the sensual magic they created between them. This was how it had always been, desire rapidly becoming a conflagration in which all the controls of civilised behaviour were swept away.

And afterwards they had lain intertwined, her head on his broad damp chest, lapped in the exquisite silken tide of satiation, and slept. Just as he had done with Gabrielle, with all the other women who found such passionate release in his arms.

With a tremendous effort she opened her eyes and said deliberately, in her most prosaic tone, 'If you plan to take me to bed now I'd better turn dinner off.'

For a moment she thought she had failed; his questing mouth moved with exquisite precision over the hollow in her throat and she shivered at the touch of his tongue on the fluttering pulse there. But then he lifted his head and there was a certain grim amusement in his eyes, as well as frustration and the smoky remnants of his passion.

'I could take you to bed and you would not resist me,' he said, and when she gave no answer he tightened his arms and said again, 'I could, Amber. Admit it.'

She winced at the raw triumph in his words, and replied dully, 'Yes, you could. But what good would it do you, beyond a brief sordid release?'

His laughter came soft and menacing. 'Oh, I think you know,' he taunted. 'There are pleasures of the mind as well as those of the body, and I have promised myself your humiliation for many years.'

But he released her, and once free from the delicious prison of his embrace she was able to summon some of the poise she had acquired over the years and say with tolerable composure, 'You don't have to keep repeating it.'

The sun had set behind the mainland and the sky was fading to a deep brilliant blue. A last cicada played its tiny zither in the trees beyond the window, was joined by the first cricket; the air was fresh and slightly scented with salt and the balsam from the tea-trees. The first star pricked a place in the fabric of the sky. With fingers that trembled Amber picked up the glass of champagne and drank a little, lowered lashes shielding her thoughts from the man who stood beside her. Desire, aching along her veins, ebbed into frustration, then subsided into a sad sweet melancholy.

She asked, 'What will you do when you go back? Set a divorce into motion?'

'I think so,' said Alex curtly. 'Then I shall marry again. This time I will choose for myself, someone I can trust not to run away if things begin to go wrong.'

'I should marry a Greek if I were you. Your women are brought up to be complaisant.'

He said between his teeth, 'And loyal.'

'And maternal,' she agreed, weary of trying to make him understand.

His shoulders moved in a shrug. 'I do not need heirs of my own body,' he said moodily, 'I have brothers and cousins. But yes, I must admit that if I am going to be a father it might as well be sooner rather than later. Do you think I will be a good father, Amber?'

The jeering note in the question made her uneasy, but she answered with cool sarcasm, 'Oh, I think you'll be marvellous—on the rare occasions when you can find time from your work and your women to visit your children. And always providing they don't learn to hate you for making their mother unhappy. It has been known to happen.'

'Do you find it so impossible to believe that I should be able to make a woman happy?'

She shrugged, each word delivered with a subtle taunting inflection. 'It astounds me that a man as intelligent and experienced as you, a man noted for his brilliance and astuteness, should understand so little about women. All that experience going for nothing! Alex, wives are possessive. Even if they marry for practical reasons most women want their husband to be faithful to them, no matter how young and beautiful and imaginative the opposition. If you don't understand that you don't know much about women.'

Obliquely he said, 'I was twenty-one when we married.'

Amber turned away and walked across to the door which led into the kitchen. 'Yes, I know. Far too young. Our fathers should have been shot. Tyrants, both of them, in different ways. Have you learned anything in the last nine years, Alex?'

He didn't raise his voice, but she heard every word he said. 'Are you interested in finding out?'

'No!' The violence of her reply startled her; she qualified it by saying hastily, 'It's no use. What's past is done with.'

His words were laced with irony. 'Haven't you learned

that the past is never done with? The future has its roots buried deep there.'

Dinner was eaten in a strained silence, broken only by Alex's smooth compliments about the food. Amber had to force it down her throat, but although champagne would have helped she dared not drink too much. It would certainly make the coming night easier for her to endure—too easy, she thought with shame, recalling her incandescent response to his kiss.

No, she would not make it easy for him. It was bad enough that he knew that she still wanted him; she wouldn't give him cause to gloat at her easy surrender. He should learn that her will was stronger than her body.

After dinner they sat opposite each other and drank coffee, she with every nerve stretched taut, he appearing completely relaxed, long legs stretched out as he watched her over the rim of the coffee cup.

Yet she sensed tension in him too, the expectant excitement of a big cat as it lies in wait for its prey. Beneath half-closed lids his eyes gleamed, cool grey warmed by little flames, and his mouth was curved into a waiting smile.

If he wanted to push her off balance he was succeeding very well. Long-forgotten pulses began to drum through her body in an overture to excitement so that she drank quickly to ease her dry mouth and throat, keeping her face averted so that he couldn't catch any more than a glimpse of the colour which burned along the elegant sweep of her cheekbones. The curl of her lashes hid the glowing heat that sparked her eyes to gold.

After a few minutes Alex said calmly, 'Do you mind if I put the television on? I believe there is an excellent documentary.'

'No, of course not.' Amber was not controlled enough to hide the relief in her voice, but although he smiled sardonically he made no comment, merely got up and opened a door in the built-in fixture along one wall to reveal the set.

Within minutes she too had become absorbed in the documentary, a brilliant but depressing evocation of life in Central America. When it was over he switched off the set and came to sit beside her, touching with a caressing finger the place where she had wiped a tear away.

'Still so easily moved?' he mocked.

'I'm afraid so. Silly, isn't it? Nick teases——'

The words were smothered by his mouth, predatory and painful. When at last he raised his head he said with molten fury, 'I do not wish to hear that name again.'

Through swollen lips she retorted, 'He exists, damn you! I can't just cut him out of my head!'

'Try,' he invited dangerously. 'I want no man's bastard in your mind when you are in my bed.'

She winced and he said with cold pleasure, 'Does it hurt to know that he can never be anything but that? If you had wanted otherwise you should have had the courage to put his father's name on the birth certificate. Or would his father not allow it?' Her astonished gasp brought a twist to his mouth. 'Yes, I have seen it. I had the faint suspicion that the child might be mine, you see, so I had a copy sent to me.'

In a voice that echoed through her mind Amber asked, 'What would you have done if he had been?'

His fingers about her chin were not painful, but there was no resisting them. Amber's lashes drooped as he surveyed her sudden pallor with chilling intensity. 'I would have taken him from you, of course. Any child of mine will be heir to much more than anything this cousin of yours can give. He would need to grow up knowing this; so many who are raised to power and wealth are not taught discipline and restraint. They sink into idleness and decadence, and let it all slip from their control. Any child of mine must be taught his duty as well as his rights.

But as your child is not mine, you and your lover are welcome to him!'

Amber drew in a deep painful breath and he smiled coldly and dropped his hand and got up. He did not move away; she could feel the icy power of his contempt oppressing her. She had to bite her lips to keep them from trembling. Thank heavens Alex did not want to discuss Nick; it was far too perilous a subject, and Alex was to astute not to realise how upset it made her. She had to ensure that his suspicions were never aroused.

But something impelled her to say in a muted, urgent voice, 'He's happy.'

'I am sure of it,' he returned with courteous indifference. There was a frigid silence before he continued, 'And you, are you happy, Amber *mou*?'

Her swift upward glance revealed nothing. He wasn't even looking at her, he was watching the flight of an unwary moth lured through the window to fly dangerously closer and closer to the lamp.

'I—yes, I'm happy,' she replied cautiously.

'Tell me what makes you so happy as mistress to this cousin?'

The pointed insolence of the question brought her head up. She said, 'Why do you want to know?'

'Because it pleases me.' His tone invested the few words with insulting contempt, but not a muscle moved in the beautiful mask of his face, and still his eyes watched the doomed moth.

Foreboding throbbed in her body. She had to swallow before she could answer, and when she did her voice was strangely husky and careful. 'I suppose it's because I'm valued.'

He waited, but she couldn't say anything else, and slowly his head turned and she met the scornful distaste of his gaze with a defiant lift of her head.

'Valued?' He made the word an obscenity. 'A whore, valued? If I had known that that was the sort of respect you wished to attain, I would have gone about things differently.'

Amber was white to the lips, but her voice firmed as she responded. 'How you love to tie labels on to people! No one else considers me a whore.'

'No? Then how do they see you?'

'Many ways,' she said carefully. 'As Nick's mother, a good one, I hope. As Matt's cousin. As a woman who pulls her weight in the district and on the station.'

'I should be interested to know how this weight is pulled,' said Alex softly. 'Does he hire you out?'

The crudity of it was like a slap in the face. She said, 'You're disgusting!'

He smiled thinly. 'Then tell me what you do that makes you so—valued.'

Proudly, her eyes hard as topazes, she told him, 'On the station I do all the bookwork, I act as Matt's secretary and I keep the records. I taught myself to type while I was pregnant and since then I've done it all, even when we decided to get a computer. I can tell anyone who asks the pedigree of almost any animal from any of the studs, or I can find it within seconds. And I act as hostess for Matt whenever he needs one, both privately and professionally, on sale days and occasions like that.'

'Fascinating,' he drawled, sarcasm abrasive in the words. 'so, you can now do the work of any little office girl.'

'And any little hostess,' she said, her voice crisp with disgust.

'And because of this you feel valued. I shall never understand women. What is so different from this life you lead here from the life you would have led as my wife?' He watched, smiling, as she froze.

She touched her tongue to suddenly dry lips. 'You already had a hostess,' she pointed out. 'Your stepmother was very definitely in charge, and she made it quite obvious that she wasn't going to take second place.'

'Would it have been so difficult to learn from her?'

Amber felt hunted. She knew that tone of wry boredom, knew from old that it was merely a cloak to conceal Alex at his most dangerous. Behind it he was watching her, waiting. She could almost see the dagger behind the silk.

'And then there was Gabrielle,' she said reluctantly.

Alex leaned back and surveyed her through half-closed eyes. 'But you are in exactly the same position here,' he drawled. 'Or did you think that this noble cousin of yours was always faithful to you?'

Something in her face made him laugh, softly, with a derisive humour. 'Poor little Amber, have I surprised you? You see, he is not so much a paragon, this handsome cousin of yours. Ever since you have been here he has had affairs. He is very discreet, but there are always people who know. You do not have much luck with your men, do you? Perhaps there is something wrong with you.'

'And perhaps,' she retorted, furious because her voice was trembling, 'perhaps there's something wrong with you. It is hardly normal to get such pleasure from poking and prying into other people's lives!'

'But you are my wife,' he taunted. 'What sort of a husband would I be if I did not do my best to see that you are happy? And how can you be happy with this cousin who is unfaithful to you, when that was the reason you left me?'

Amber's teeth sank into her bottom lip. She made to get up, jerking herself away from the knowing perception in his eyes, but his hands clamped on to her wrist and held her in place.

'Tell me,' he insisted silkily.

She said desperately, 'I won't tell you anything. You have no right to know.'

'Why do you stay with him when you left me?' he

demanded with a return to the contemptuous insolence she dreaded.

'Perhaps because I love him.'

His hand on her chin was brutal, jerking her face around to meet his. 'Do you?' he demanded, and when she gave him nothing but mute resistance he said between his teeth, 'Tell me! Or I will spend all night cracking through that shell that surrounds your brain.'

Sullenly, driven by fear to a lie that was only half a lie, she shouted, 'Yes, I do—I love him!'

Alex flung her from him, hissing through his teeth. He stood up with less than his usual grace and stood watching her, his fierce implacable face dark as a demon's mask.

'So,' he said. 'I think it is time for bed. Come.'

The colour drained from her skin, then returned in a shaming surge. In a stifled voice she began to protest, but his bright merciless stare silenced her, and after a moment she got stiffly to her feet. Telling herself that Nick's safety was worth anything, even complete loss of pride, she preceded Alex into the bedroom. His hand rested in the small of her back; there was hardly any pressure and no force at all, but the warmth of it burnt through the thin silk of her dress like a brand.

The bedroom too overlooked the bay and the sea beyond it. Silver light lay like a benediction over the water, romantic, beautiful, but the full moon had risen behind the house and the room was dark. Alex switched on the light and walked across to pull the curtains over the windows.

'Later,' he told her coolly, once more in complete control, 'I shall pull them back. Perhaps you may not recall that when I can I like to sleep with the windows open to the night. But for now, I do not want any passing yachtsman to enjoy a striptease.'

He sat down on the side of the enormous bed, examining her appalled expression with savage enjoy-

ment. 'Well, my dear,' he said at last, after silence had
lengthened into tension, 'undress for me.'

Sudden shocking tears enlarged her already enormous
eyes. She said urgently, 'Alex, there's not need to
humiliate me any further.'

'Why not?' His dark uplifted brows taunted her. 'I
remember a touching shyness when we were first
married, but there is no need to pretend now. You have
had nine years to become accustomed to undressing for a
man. Show me how you titillate this cousin of yours.' He
stretched back on to the pillows, smiling, his face carved
into lines of ruthless purpose.

She said, 'No.'

He laughed softly. 'I shall have to force you, then.'

Fear gave a kick in her stomach but she said
stubbornly, 'Very well, you can rip the clothes of my back
if that's what you want, but you can't force me to undress
in front of you like some—some harem girl.'

She expected an explosion of quick anger, even fury;
Alex was not accustomed to being defied. Adored since
childhood, loved and spoiled by his father and both his
long-dead mother and the stepmother who had taken her
place, he demanded instant compliance with his wishes.
Only a character as controlled and as strong-willed as his
would have been able to endure such a start in life
without warping.

But instead of the deadly anger Amber expected he
merely laughed and swung himself off the bed and came
towards her, handsome as a Greek god, his mouth curved
in a smile as old as the Greek hills.

'So defiant,' he murmured as he reached her. 'And so
beautiful.'

His reaction astonished her. Too astounded to resist
the downward swoop of his mouth, she stood passively,
and then it was too late, because the sensual magic he
created for her had her in its spell.

Stiff and still in his embrace, she neither responded to

nor fought the softly impatient touch of his mouth on hers, and after a moment he lifted his head and she breathed again, hoping that he had given up. But he had merely changed tack. The calculated warmth of his mouth moved to her eyes, sealing them, and then across to her temple, touching the vulnerable hollow with something close to tenderness. She flinched, because this was what she feared; she could have dealt with rape, with crude force, but seduction was another matter, and of course he was too clever not to know it.

Fleetingly she wondered why he had not used his power over her to insist on the striptease; if he had said that Matt's future depended on it she would have done it, because she owed more to her cousin than she could ever repay.

But before she could follow the thought through his mouth closed on the soft lobe of her ear, and she had to fight down a tiny whimpering noise in her throat. Until then his hands had stayed chastely across her back; now, as his tongue explored the curves and whorls of her ear they hardened into fetters, holding her imprisoned against the vaunting virility she so feared.

She said, 'No, oh no,' babbling, because she could not think, because the warmth of his breath in her ear and the gentle exploration of his tongue were combining with the hard arousal of his body to send her burning into that region where all else was forgotten but hunger and need and the turbulent demands of her sensual self.

CHAPTER FOUR

'ALEX,' she groaned, terrified by this open betrayal of her desire.

'Hush, my little dove, my sweet eyes, don't argue, don't think . . .'

Shuddering, the rigours sensitising her aching body, her hands crept up from her side and wound themselves about his neck. She gloated at the heat in his skin, the dampness that betrayed his passion, and slid her fingers into the black crisp curls at the nape of his neck, stroking with a delicate touch as his tongue stabbed into the depths of her ear.

Another groan forced its way up her closed throat. She gasped for air and her hips began to move, slightly yet with inborn provocation in a rhythm as primitive and as old as male and female, coaxing, supplicating, promising all the delights of a forbidden paradise.

Alex muttered something in French and those possessive hands slid the length of her back, pressing and urging, as his mouth opened over hers and he made himself master of her responses. He was braced and ready, the narrow hips and wide shoulders rigid with desire. When Amber moved with sensuous grace against him she was responding to the explosive tension in his every muscle and sinew, and beneath his her mouth shaped a siren's smile, alluring, blindly offering the satiation of his hunger in the sweet heated depths of her body.

'Touch me,' he ordered harshly. 'I am mad for you, I want your hands to learn to know me again.'

Her lashes fluttered up so that her eyes met the burning, devouring darkness of his, and she ripped his shirt open, uncaring of the material. He was magnificent, tanned and smooth, skin like heated, oiled silk covering a muscular strength which should have terrified her. With a desperate little moan she pressed open-mouthed kisses to his shoulders and over the width of his chest, glorying in the clenching of the muscles beneath.

'My lovely one,' he whispered, half laughing, half on a groan, 'ah, Amber, give me the same delights I have offered you. I want to see your beautiful body, feel the beat of your heart against mine ...'

The little dress slid easily over her shoulders and on to the floor and she was left in the teddy, so transparent and fragile that it was as though she had nothing on. Through the pale material her skin gleamed ivory gold, warm and beckoning and rich, her small breasts not needing the support of the silk.

'And how does this pretty thing come off?' Alex asked deep in his throat, running a questing hand from her throat to the hard peak of one breast.

Amber couldn't think. Her whole brain had turned into nothing more than a receptacle for the messages from her nerve ends, the incredible sweep of sensation through her body, the urgent, almost painful demands it imposed on her, the surge of hunger and delight that raced through every cell. She kissed the pulse in his throat, her own leaping in time, and sensuously, delicately as a cat, licked a bead of sweat from his shoulder.

Somehow, she never knew how, the teddy was lowered to waist level, and his mouth moved to plunder the soft curves of her breast while one hand slid lower, and touched and pressed. Trembling, unable to speak, she clung to him with febrile passion, holding his head to her breast, shaking with need as the molten heat of his mouth enclosed the sensitive nub. Sensation, pure as crystal, stabbed through her body, transfixed her with rapture.

She must have moaned something because he lifted his

head and smiled into her dazzled face and whispered, 'Take it off, my heart, my siren.'

And something in his face, something buried deep in the dilated blackness of his eyes, perhaps a twist of the lips which had so sweetly suckled on her a moment ago, betrayed him.

She whispered, 'You *bastard*!' and tried to stiffen her limbs enough to fight free.

No longer caressing, with the power of fulfilment in their fingertips, his hands turned cruel, tearing the remnants of the little teddy from her shrinking form, and when he had done that he demanded with vicious irony, 'Who won, do you think? Shall we say honours even?'

His eyes swept the length of her body. Deep in his chest his breath caught harshly; he still wanted her, but the clamour in his body was being subdued by that iron will, and after a moment he flung her away and said harshly, 'Get into bed.'

Shocked and icy cold, Amber was shivering, her body raw with need. She stood staring numbly at him, and he swore beneath his breath and picked her up and dumped her on to the bed, dragging up the sheet to cover her as though he couldn't bear to see her.

The light snapped off; she heard the swish of the curtains being drawn free of the windows, a rustle as he removed the rest of his clothes, and then the side of the mattress dipped and for the first time in nine years she was sharing a bed.

Rigid as a board, hardly daring to breathe, she lay waiting for his onslaught, but he stayed strictly on his side and made no attempt to turn her way, and after long minutes she realised incredulously that he was not going to make love to her.

The whole tempestuous episode had been coldly, ruthlessly calculated. Alex had wanted to show her that he could use the merciless attraction that existed between them to persuade her into doing anything, and having proved his point he was going to sleep. Once more she had seen the violence in him, the dark side of his nature which he was able to harness to his determination. It was this intense driving force which made him so brilliant a businessman—and so feared a man. He was never sidetracked, he had no self-indulgent weaknesses which got in the way of his aims. It was no wonder his family regarded him with awe, no wonder his adversaries feared him, no wonder that governments treated him with respect.

As she lay stiffly beside him Amber told herself that it would be fatal to believe he was invulnerable. He was just a man, not, perhaps, as other men, but not so very different, either. He had weaknesses, if only she could find them. And he had the devil's own nerve to treat her as though she were a lesser form of life.

I'll show you, she thought savagely, welcoming the anger with desperation, using it to wipe away the shame and the lingering ache of desire which corroded the fragile fabric of her composure

But her anger only lasted a short time. She was not like him, able to put it on hold until she had the chance to exorcise it.

Now, when she needed it, it ebbed away, leaving her with the acrid taste of apprehension in her mouth. He was a cruel swine, implacable in his need for revenge, and he had shown her how he was going to make her pay for what he saw as her betrayal all those years ago. With her body and her pride, and of those two, it was her pride he wanted to humble most. The corrosive frustration which was even now eating into her nerves was only the start. He wanted her so hungry that she would do almost anything, surrender all that she had won, her independence, her self-possession, to satisfy her need for the sensual oblivion he held so tantalisingly just out of reach.

And her blood ran cold, because she knew that when she was broken, he would laugh in her face and leave her.

That would be his revenge.

For long minutes she lay listening to his deep slow breathing, measuring it against the tender hush of the waves on the little beach below, and gradually realised that it was altogether too even, too deep. She remembered other nights when she had lain wakeful and bitter beside him; he had been a restless sleeper, turning as if that magnificent body and brain were never entirely at repose. His breathing had altered cadence quite often.

So unless he had managed to unlearn the habits of a lifetime, he too was lying awake in the quiet of the night. Fiercely, angrily satisfied, the smile that widened her mouth was not pleasant. She toyed with the idea of making advances towards him, and then rejecting him as he had her, but common sense banished that idea very quickly. She had no illusions about Alex; he would think nothing of taking her, and he would make sure that it happened in the most humiliating way possible. And when it came to humiliation, Alex was an expert.

No, much better to leave him aching with the same need that stretched her body taut on a rack of unsatisfied desire.

Smiling sardonicaly, she drifted off to sleep.

And awoke to another beautiful day, the early sun still hidden behind the bulk of the island, but its rays dancing over the glittering waters of the bay, gilding the mainland so that it glowed like some celestial country, the promised land, the land of lost delights.

Beside her Alex muttered something in Greek, and groaned; she froze, then turned slowly, her breath painful in her throat, to look at him.

Even the unconsciousness of sleep couldn't hide the predatory strength of his features. She was reminded of the many Greek statues she had seen with their starkly classical perfection of feature and form, strength allied to beauty. It was incredible that after two and half thousand years the type should still be so prevalent, for Alex was not alone in his stunning attractiveness. There were many others in his country who pleasured the eye as he did, although Amber had seen none with the same combination of passion and control stamped in their features.

She held her breath as he turned his head slightly; his lashes flickered and he frowned, but only for a second until his face resumed the calm impersonality of sleep, and the breath hissed softly from her lungs.

Lashes like fur, thick and innocent against the bronze of his cheek, concealing eyes which were sharply intelligent, yet the veneer of beauty could not hide the power and force of the man.

Remembering that he had always been amorous in the mornings, Amber slid slowly and stealthily from the bed. Remembering, too, that in spite of the cut-throat world in which he functioned, Alex had a Greek appreciation of the simple things of life. Like dancing, and drinking, and eating, and the soft pleasures of a woman's body. Any woman, provided she was beautiful.

And with the superb body and the brilliant mind and the direct sensual appreciation went other attitudes, just as simple, just as primitive, like vengefulness, and cruelty, and an icy, determined willpower.

Moving quietly as a cat, she went through into the dressing-room and slid open a drawer in which she was sure she had seen swimwear the day before. But she was wrong, for all that was in there were bikini pants.

Irritated, she jerked open other drawers, but something niggled at the back of her mind, and she came back to the first drawer, pulling out a silk concoction, holding it at arm's length as she frowned over it.

Her mouth tightened as she finally caught the wisp of recollection. In those hectic months between her engagement and her marriage when she had been taken around the couture houses shopping for clothes by Alex's stepmother, they had bought exquisite underwear in a shop in Paris, and there she had seen just such items.

The saleswoman had been amused at her naïve interest, and shown them to her, smiling when Irene had said, 'No, not for you, Amber.'

'Why not?'

The two older women had exchanged glances, and it was the saleswoman who had explained. 'These are to swim in,' she said, hiding her amusement. 'They are for men who need to be——' she had paused delicately, her black eyes snapping, '——excited. Monsieur Stephanides is not such a one. At his age he will be ardent, eager.'

Amber had been embarrassed, as much by Irene's open amusement as by the flimsy little garments, which was probably why the incident had remained in her mind.

Now she knew exactly what they were. For a long moment she stood with one of the pretty decadent things twisted in her hands, her mouth tight beneath bleak, suddenly tired eyes. She might just as well wear nothing. But as she put it back a sudden gleam arrested her misery. How often she had read that nakedness was not nearly so arousing as the erotic promise of it?

Was it true? Her expression hardened; she didn't know why, but she would feel less humiliated naked than wearing a flimsy little *cache-sexe* chosen to underline Alex's caustic contempt. She could carry off nakedness with pride.

For a moment she hesitated, wondering if she had the courage, wondering if he would see her nudity as an invitation and a surrender, but pride stiffened her shoulders. He was extremely perceptive; he would know what she was doing, and her resistance would make her feel better.

Defiantly she tiptoed into his bathroom and slid into the robe behind the door, collected a towel, then crept out of the house and made her way through the wet dew to the beach. Once there she walked across the warming crispness of the sand to the shade of the pohutukawa tree, standing in its protection while she wondered if she had been incredibly stupid. Perhaps it would be better to go back to the house . . .

But the sea gleamed an invitation, and why should she creep around like a mouse hunted by a cat? Her shoulders lifted. Moving with conscious grace, she draped both the towel and the robe over a convenient twig and stepped out of the shade to run down through the glorious gold and blue morning.

The sand was damp beneath her feet; she welcomed the shock of the water with pleasure, because it stopped the forbidden stirrings of her body.

Swimming naked was a sheer delight, a sybaritic yielding to all that was unfettered and free in her nature. Normally she would have revelled in the flow of water over her limbs and the sleek pale skin of her body, but as she swam lazily across the bay she was soon lost in angry speculation about Alex's motives. Was he going to taunt her again and again with her weakness where he was concerned? It seemed likely, and she respected his willpower enough to realise that he would be able to control his own desires with a ruthless rein while using his sexuality to force her capitulation.

She dived to the sandy bottom, her eyes mutinous as she scooped up a shell. No, she was damned if she was going to submit to that kind of emotional terrorism. If he wanted to play dirty she could too. How would he respond if instead of fighting him she deliberately succumbed, and used all her allure to get him into bed?

It would be a difficult part for her to play, that of temptress. But at least, if she did, his plan would backfire, especially if he weakened and they ended up making love.

The shell was deceptively fragile, a semi-circle of pale gold mother-of-pearl, translucent and pure. Amber held it cupped in her fingers, watching the opalescent play of sunlight on its crinkled surface; her jaw set and she clenched her hand, opening it just before the fine pretty thing cut the skin.

A movement on shore snapped her head up. Alex was coming down the path, the sun playing over his body with the complacent caress of a lover. He wore brief black trunks and had a towel slung over his shoulder. For a moment Amber's breath was stifled in her lungs; he looked like one of the gods on his way to dally with the nearest nereid. Her eyes swung reluctantly back to the frail glowing shell in her hand and she firmed her mouth, her mind made up.

So be it. If he was looking forward to seducing a reluctant wife, she would be far from reluctant. She would aspire to a worldliness she knew she would never attain; she would be flirtatious and cheerfully amorous, and she would make it quite clear that when he went she would return to her life with Matt without a pang.

If that didn't infuriate him and destroy his pleasure in his schemes, she had forgotten what the man was like!

Her hand opened. She dropped the shell and dived under the water again, summoning as much composure as she could, and trying hard to ignore the nasty little voice that whispered that no one played games with Alex Stephanides—especially after the first one.

If his plans were proceeding nicely he wasn't revealing it. The sunlight played across a face as impassive as a statue's, picking out the arrogant strength of line and plane. Amber trod water as he walked into the sea, watching gravely as he dived beneath the water to emerge very close to her. He didn't look astonished at her cheerful greeting, although his eyes narrowed momentarily. the sun gleamed on his head as he responded formally, 'Good morning. You slept well.'

'Like a log,' she said blithely, adding, 'You looked very peaceful. Have you been overworking lately?'

Yes, he didn't like to think that she had watched him

in his sleep. Some unknown emotion glittered beneath his lids, but he answered, 'A little. I tried to get as much done as possible so that there would be little to intrude on this second honeymoon.'

His tone invested the last few words with the sharp bite of sarcasm. Amber grinned. 'If you think this is anything like a honeymoon you're a romantic,' she taunted maddeningly, and dived, unable to cope with the sight of so much bronzed and gleaming flesh.

He caught her within a few seconds, his hand on her arm urging her up through the sunlit water to the surface, and held her there, his grey gaze searching her face with merciless assessment.

'You look almost mischievous,' he said slowly. 'Why, I wonder?'

'Perhaps because it's a glorious morning,' she offered. 'Or because this is the first holiday I've had for some years.'

'Holiday? What do you do that keeps you so busy you need a holiday?'

She reacted to the jeering note in his voice with a quick anger, hastily hidden, but she could have cursed at the flare of satisfaction she saw in his eyes.

'I work quite hard,' she said deliberately. 'The station can't compare with the Stephanides Corporation, of course, but there's enough work to need a secretary, and that's what I am.'

The satisfaction turned into disbelief. 'I find it difficult to believe that you enjoy doing such work.'

She smiled patiently. 'That's because you've always thought I'm an idiot. I'm not, you know. I'm quite capable of using a computer.'

'You and any other little office girl,' said Alex in cruel disparagement, adding cynically, 'But your work is not so necessary that your absence will cause any problems.'

The waves lifted them a few inches, let them down gently, and because they were both out of their depth, the pressure of the tide eased their legs together. Amber gave a wild little shudder, and so that he wouldn't notice said crisply, 'Everything is under control. I've paid all the bills for this month and everything else can wait. Like you, I can work long hours to catch up.'

He smiled oddly. 'But we have years to catch up,' he said, deliberately tangling her legs with his as he pulled her into the cool length of his body.

Amber caught her breath, alarmed at the arc of fire that streaked between them. The smile on his mouth eased into something more impersonal yet more intimate, hardening into lines of passion.

'Years and years,' he murmured, watching her as his hand came up to the wet smooth globe of her breast.

His eyes darkened. Beneath his fingers the nipple flowered, as blatant as the virility he could not hide. Sunlight glittered on Amber's lashes, creating a rainbow, a prism of radiance, and she said something, the words floating through the warm salt-spiced air, insubstantial as bubbles.

Alex smiled and slid his hand from her breast up to her throat, long fingers tightening for just long enough to make her catch her breath, then he laughed and picked her up and held her upright out of the water, his satyr's face pagan and fierce in the sun, before he buried his face in the taut flatness of her stomach. She gasped and grabbed the wet black curls, trying to tear his face away, but the muscles in his neck stood out bullishly, and whatever she did she could not wrench his mouth from its erotic, leisurely exploration of her navel.

Only when she was hot and pulsing with desire did he slide her the full length of his body, holding her with brutal lack of finesse against him so that she was assailed by the blatant hunger he did not try to hide. Mutely she stared up into his mocking face, automatically noting the signs that signalled arousal, the dilated darkness in the centres of his eyes and the dark flush outlining his cheekbones, the curve of his mouth, sensual and yet tightly disciplined.

As if her survey was an intrusion he watched her a long, tense moment with half-closed eyes before opening his arms to let her float free.

Amber said tightly, 'I'd better go up and get breakfast.'

'No, stay here.' It was an order, not a suggestion.

Striving hard to regain some of the equanimity he had wrested from her with that little bit of provocative byplay, she shrugged and turned away, swimming for the raft. He made no attempt to come after her, but as she sat there watching him swim she was not fooled. She was as much his prisoner as if he had her chained to a wall, and he enjoyed forcing her to accept it.

Pride demanded that she hold her head high. Alex had a hidden contempt for women; he had loved his gentle mother but respected and admired his dominating father who had been born, lived and died a chauvinist. After the tragically early death of Alex's mother old Nikos had married again, solely for more sons. There had been three, and two daughters, whom he had married to advantage, but he had left the control of his estate to the son who resembled him most.

His second wife was still alive, a woman whose smile hid malice. Irene liked shopping and displaying her jewellery, entertaining her friends and spoiling her sons.

At first Amber had tried to become friends with her, but Irene was fiercely possessive of her position and had made it quite clear to Amber that she was not wanted, not in the villa, not in Irene's life at all. It had been an impossible situation; from the vantage point of nine extra years Amber realised that nothing she could have done would have won Irene over, but at the time she had been hurt by yet another rejection. And she had learned to despise Alex because he had been angry when she complained, telling her that she would have to learn to live with his stepmother. That had been a rejection too. It was then that she had realised that, like her father, he didn't really care whether or not she was happy. Coupled with his behaviour over Gabrielle, and the shattering realisation that he wasn't going to give the French-woman up, she had been devastated.

Now, when her emotions were no longer involved, she could see that his behaviour was on a par with his unspoken contempt for women. He abrogated to himself the right to punish her for her supposed adultery, yet he had expected her to accept his women, his lifestyle, without protest because he was a man.

The double standard, she thought ironically as she pushed her wet curls back from her face, was new-minted and fresh-forged each time a boy-child was born in Greece. But at least Nick was safe from its crippling effects. Or as safe as she could make him, she thought with a certain mordant humour, recalling some chauvin-ist attitudes still rampant in New Zealand. Not even Matt was immune.

But it wasn't taken entirely for granted, as it was in Greece, where the dowry, the payment made by one family to another to sweeten the acquisition of a wife, was also still alive and flourishing.

The dowry made her wonder calmly what had happened to hers, the bribe that her father had paid out. Lord, but she'd been naïve! She felt sorry for the seventeen-year-old child who had innocently believed in love and the right to happiness.

But surely one was entitled to be a little naïve at seventeen? Surely all girls did not have to grow up as quickly and roughly as she had. As for the power, the promise of control over her father's business empire which had persuaded Alex to marry her, she wasn't interested. She had grown up with money and power; she knew, none better, that they didn't bring happiness. Too much money was as dangerous as too little; it was much better for Nick to make his own life than be saddled with an inheritance which could lead to indulgence of the worst sort.

'What are you thinking?'

She looked down into his face, her reluctant eyes appreciating the picture he made. A strong forearm rested along the edge of the raft, the dark fine hair already drying in the sun. As he moved, exerting pressure, the muscles flexed eloquently beneath the warm skin; he hauled himself up beside her, water streaming in a veil over his splendidly sculpted form.

Amber dragged her bemused eyes away to watch a gannet dive into the water beyond the reef, envying it its freedom. It was, of course, an illusion; the bird was bound just as immutably by instinct as she was by the ties of the body and the heart. To Nick, with a fierce protective maternal instinct, to Matt because he was her best friend, to the man who stretched out beside her with the splendid ease of a great cat, because she had married him and borne his child.

'Tell me,' he insisted lazily. 'You looked—oh, half angry, yet very determined.'

She smiled. 'Did I? I was wondering what had happened to my father's estate.'

'It all came to me,' he said drily. 'You were not mentioned in the will.'

She nodded, not at all surprised. 'He wanted a son. I'm glad he finally got what he wanted.'

'You could apply to have the will revoked.' Alex was watching her with the clear scalpel-sharp regard of a master surgeon. 'As his child you are entitled to a share.'

Her smooth honey-gold shoulders moved in a slight shrug. 'Money means nothing—well, very little. You're welcome to it. My father hated me the day I was born because I wasn't a son, and when he realised that I'd managed to damage my mother so much that she couldn't have any more children, his hatred increased each year that went past. As a child I was convinced that there was something drastically wrong with me, that I was horrifically ugly, because he couldn't even bear to look at me. I loved my mother and my nanny because I thought they were wonderful to be able to look at me without showing their revulsion. I must have been about ten when I realised that it wasn't my face he couldn't bear, it was me.'

Her voice was light, but he put out a hand and took hers, holding it for a moment in a grip which had nothing more to it than the sympathy of one human being for another. As he released it he said drily, 'You should have been born to a Greek family, Amber. Our children are our treasures. If he wanted a son so much it was a wonder he did not divorce your mother and marry again.'

His understanding left her feeling somehow exposed, raw and wary. She did not want to like him, to have him reveal himself as a man who could feel for a bewildered child caught in a hell not of her own making. Deliberately she summoned the memory of the emotions she had felt when she realised that he was not going to give up the beautiful Frenchwoman who had shared so many nights with him.

In an acid voice she said, 'In some strange frightening way I think he must have loved her. He treated her like dirt, yet when he did suggest a divorce so that he could father those sons he wanted so desperately, he wanted her to be his mistress. She told him that if he divorced her he would never see her again, so he gave up the idea. Of course, he made her pay every subsequent day of her life for refusing him.'

Alex said quite gently, 'She must have loved him also.'

'If she did, she was crazy.' Pain for her mother made her reckless and forgetful. 'God, I wouldn't let a man do that to me!'

'So I found out,' he said, caustic mockery edging his voice. 'You were too frightened to permit a man to do anything to you! A silly weak little adolescent who ran at the first sign of trouble.'

The injustice of it stung her into an unwise response. 'It wasn't the first sign,' she said acidly. 'I ran when I managed to struggle through the romantic mist I'd conjured up about me and understood at last that I was just a convenience. I saw what a life like that did to my mother, I wasn't going to spend the rest of my life waiting for you to come home after sleeping with an assortment of girl friends.'

She turned and looked down at him, at the broad back and narrow waist, the tight masculine buttocks beneath the thin material of his trunks and the long, heavily muscled legs. A pang of desire almost tore her in two so that she had to wait a moment before she could steady her voice enough to finish, 'You must know how it feels, Alex. You said I made a fool of you—well, not until you made a laughing stock of me!'

He had been lying with his face pillowed on his arms, eyes closed against the brilliance of the sun on the sea. Now he sat up and pulled her roughly across the raft to a foot or so away from him, holding her by the wrists. His eyes leaped, disconcerting her, but he asked calmly enough, 'Was that why you left me? To pay me back?'

Amber shrugged. She was not going to reveal the secrets of her poor little adolescent heart for his unkind amusement. 'Why not? We have a saying, what's sauce for the goose is sauce for the gander. I don't really see why you're so angry. After all, you got what you wanted, more power, more money, any woman you care to take. Nine years ago you didn't consider your marriage to be important enough to give up even one of those things for. I find it rather difficult to believe that you suffered so much pain that you have to seek revenge for it.'

His grip on her arms tightened. He snarled, 'But you do not understand anything, do you? You are still the foolish little girl who let Irene humiliate her in her own home, who ran crying at the first setback, who refused to even fight for her marriage! Your vows meant nothing to you!'

'My vows meant as much to me as yours did to you!' she spat back, deliberately and untruthfully.

His hands relaxed. He lifted them and looked down at the white marks, now filling with colour, and made a soft little sound. 'Ah,' he said, bending to put his mouth against the abused skin, 'I am sorry, Amber. See, I will kiss them better . . .'

She pulled away, but he jerked her off balance and she found herself lying across his lap, his warm persuasive mouth tenderly smoothing over the marks. Her breath rasped painfully in her lungs, a tight knot forming under her heart; Amber realised that she was holding her breath and forced herself to release it, to fix her eyes on a speedboat tearing across to the mainland, to ignore the black head so close to her breasts and the sweet touch of his tongue across her skin.

Desire clutched her stomach in its torrid grip. She exclaimed, 'No!' and tried to pull away, but her limbs wouldn't move and she obeyed limply as he spread her down on to the raft, her breath coming in shallow pants through lips slack and tender.

He muttered, 'So beautiful. Slender as a dryad . . .' His mouth moved to the indentation of her waist, and she rediscovered just how potent a man's kiss could be against the smooth perfection of her skin. Hunger pulsed through her in heated waves of sensation, drugging, infinitely rousing, and yet she could not move.

The sun gilded her long legs and the sweet high curves of her breasts, so that when at last Alex's head blocked out its rays she made a small sound of protest. He was smiling, the taut, angry smile of a man caught in the web of unwanted desire, and he said through his teeth, 'Touch me, Amber. I want you to touch me.'

It took all her willpower to shake her head. She could not resist this golden tide of sensation, but she could stop

herself surrendering to it. So though the tips of her
fingers tingled with an urgent need to discover the
contours of his splendid body, she let them lie laxly by her
side, and beneath the long gilded lashes her expression
was one of stony resistance.

His face tightened into a mask of anger. 'Damn you!'
he whispered. 'I know you're not frigid! Give me what I
want, you little bitch!'

She said through stiff lips, 'What do you want?'

His mouth swooped on to the curve of her breast,. 'I
want what you give your lover,' he said grimly. 'I want
you. All of you, mine for as long as I want you. I am going
to see your beautiful calm face pleading with me to take
you, and I am going to take you in every way there is. I
want to sate myself in this lovely treacherous body until I
can look at you without feeling anything but disgust. And
when I've done that I'll send you back to your lover and
tell him what we've done, and then we will see if he wants
you back!'

Anger and revulsion roiled in her stomach, but she
didn't dare move. There had been a note of bitter
determination in his voice which frightened her; he was
dangerous, almost uncontrolled, and she didn't know
how to deal with him. She had never seen him like this
before.

The hunger in his eyes had faded to another need,
another desire, more dangerous than simple passion; she
stayed still as he lay with his cheek on the soft mound of
her breast, his big body tensed and challenging. It was
almost as though he was bracing himself for some test.

Wearily, she asked, 'Is revenge so important to you,
Alex?'

He laughed and sat up, his eyes very bright and hard.
'Amber *mou*, for nine years this revenge has been a little
pleasure I promised myself whenever I wondered
whether it was worth working so hard with only brothers
to pass on my inheritance to. Nine years is a long time,

and the pleasure of my revenge has increased in a direct ratio for every one of those years. I've waited too long to leave you without achieving my goal. Only when I have had my fill of you will I divorce you and marry again, and make myself some children.'

The brutal statement ran jagged across Amber's nerves. She flinched, and his eyes brightened, that cold little smile making his mouth a frighteningly merciless slash in the dark contours of his face.

'Does that frighten you?' he asked softly, watching her with the relaxed menacing confidence of a panther which sees an antelope in its range.

'Oh, yes.' Her voice was shaking, but she met his eyes without evasion. 'I don't understand such stubborn hatred.'

He grinned, but his eyes were still cold, almost speculative. 'I find that strange. By your own admission your family was a tangle of repressions and dark, twisted emotions. Your father had to be the coldest man I have ever met.'

Fear and distaste ran chill like a shudder across her skin. 'Yes. Is it any wonder I tried to steer clear of complications? My mother was so unhappy, all her life.' She shivered. 'And I don't suppose my father was very happy, either.'

Amber sat up, using the movement to get away from him. 'I used to think that if you loved someone you wanted them to be happy. Simple, and easy. But if what my father felt for my mother was love, then I want nothing of it.'

'Your mother should not have spoken of this to you.' Incredibly, Alex sounded angry. 'How old were you when she died? Only sixteen, wasn't it? You were a child, too young to have that sort of twisted relationship dumped on to you.'

She laughed, caught her breath and laughed again, with wry, unamused fervour. 'Too young for that, but only a year later you didn't think I was too young to learn that my husband had no intention of being faithful to me, and that he didn't care a hoot whether or not I was unhappy in the house he brought me to.'

A faint note of hysteria warned her and she stopped, blinking ferociously, appalled to discover that the pain was still there. How could she blame Alex for his desire to be revenged, if the anguish she thought she had overcome years ago was still present, lurking like an unwelcome visitor in the shadows of her life?

'Perhaps I expected too much,' he said curtly, further astounding her. 'But at least I did not run away. I was prepared to try hard at our marriage, find ways to make it work.'

She couldn't let herself laugh again, or the underlying hysteria would burst through. Instead she said with a sudden savage bitterness, 'Yes, provided you didn't have to give up anything, your mistress, your pleasant life on your island with your stepmother and everyone in the villa rushing around to obey your every whim, the women who flocked around you whenever you went out into the world. You wanted it all, Alex, and you have the nerve to be angry with me because *I* wanted a little more from you than clothes and jewels and the occasional moments you could spare me from work and women, and your immense generosity in allowing me the occasional use of your body to get me pregnant!'

She spat the last words at him as if they were stones from a slingshot, uncaring of the darkening storm signals in his eyes and the harsh clenching of his face, finishing with contempt, 'And a pretty shopworn body at that, one that's known almost every pretty woman it's seen!'

She was a fool, but he had always been able to abrade the raw nerves that fed her temper. He was the only person to have this effect on her; normally she was calm and placid. As she should have been then.

While the red glow of her temper faded she tilted her

chin, frightened at the reaction her taunt caused. His mouth tightened into a thin, scornfully arrogant line and with cold eyes he scanned the defiant outrage in her expression.

'That,' he said as he pushed her down on to the raft, 'was a challenge. I enjoy challenges, Amber, especially those I know I can meet and win.'

CHAPTER FIVE

SHE SAID, 'No!' but Alex laughed, a humourless sound from deep in his throat, and pinned her to the platform with a cruel hand on each elbow as his mouth came down on her throat. Amber glared into the bright sky, her eyes sparking fury, and he muttered against the cool damp satin of her skin, 'This is what you wanted.'

'No!'

'You are lying. Why else would you swim as naked as a goddess? There are plenty of bathing suits for you at the house.'

His mouth was barely touching her skin, but she felt the soft movements far more acutely than the grip of his fingers.

'Because I didn't like them,' she said aggressively. 'They're vulgar—like all the clothes you've bought me. Cheap and nasty and vulgar.'

He laughed and kissed the corner of her mouth. 'Not cheap, I can assure you. And I would have thought, although I must admit that a woman's mind is not the most logical of things, that it was less embarrassing for you to wear clothes of my providing, however vulgar, than to go naked.'

'I don't think so.' Amber tried to project a flat, confident tone, but she could not prevent the tremor that nullified her intention to show him how unaffected she was by his lovemaking. 'I'm not ashamed of my body, but those—those *things* pander to a nasty covert voyeurism.'

He laughed again, his breath warm across her skin, and taunted, 'Think that if it makes you feel better, but if you were truly afraid of surrendering you would wear anything rather than permit me to see you as you are now. Not that I am complaining, I enjoy sharing my house with a nymph who glories in the lovely nakedness of her body.'

She wondered wildly what to say. Was he right, was her refusal to wear the *cache-sexe* based on a hidden desire to succumb to him?

Her teeth scored her lip, but she said cautiously, 'I honestly didn't think you'd come down . . .' Alex lifted his head a little and angry colour swept up from her throat at the smiling disbelief in his face. 'I don't like it,' she said again, humiliated and furious. 'I won't be treated as an object, a body to be displayed for your titillation!'

The smile turned into laughter, deep and menacing in that sparkling, glowing air. 'Oh yes, you will, because that is all you are. An instrument for my pleasure,' he said, and lowered his head and forced her head back on to the raft in a kiss that spoke of nothing but stark possession.

When she was gasping for breath he lifted his head and ran a hard, purposeful hand down her throat and across her shoulder, stopping just before the burgeoning softness of her breast. He watched her with dark, hooded eyes, enjoying the outrage she couldn't hide, and the uneasy excitement which struggled for life in her expression.

'How many times do I have to tell you?' he said clearly. 'While you are here you are my toy, my plaything. Whatever I want you to do, you will do, or your lover will suffer.'

His teeth closed very gently on the slight mound of her breast. Amber hated herself for the shiver which roughened the surface of her skin, but managed to choke back the high wild little sound that fought for release in her throat.

The sun beat down, golden and fierce, summoning an

answering heat from the primal source deep inside her body. It was humiliating to want him; perhaps she should have had affairs in the years they had been parted, so that she was blasé and experienced, so accustomed to the tender rasp of a man's breath against her skin as his mouth explored her that it meant little beyond a pleasant relief of urges long indulged.

Only she had never wanted another man, not even Matt who was handsome and vital and very, very attractive. Somehow, possibly because she had been so young when they married, her body's reactions were attuned only to this man.

And he would take her to appease his stark need for revenge.

She stiffened, her skin flaming as his tongue dipped into the tight hollow of her navel, and said in a flat controlled voice, 'Are you going to make love here? Because there's a yacht appearing between the islands, heading this way.'

Alex stopped, and turned his head so that he could see out to sea. For a moment he lay with his face against her stomach, his lean hard strength sprawled solid and warm across her legs, and for that moment time seemed to stand still. The raft lifted and fell with gentle regularity in the soft wash of the waves. Water gurgled pleasantly past on its way to the little pink beach; above the sound was another, the harsh, evocative music of the cicadas in the trees, and an incongruously cheerful call from a blackbird.

Amber lay supine, pinned to the raft by the weight of a man who was toying with her body and her emotions and her pride, and all that she could think of was that she felt oddly satisfied beneath him, conscious of the rise and fall of his chest, the faint roughness of his beard against the skin of her stomach lending a sharp *frisson* of pleasure.

I must be decadent, she thought, defying such unwanted unexpected delight, and he sighed and said,

'You are right. We had better go where no one can watch us.'

He made her walk ahead of him up the path because, he told her jeeringly, the sight of her small slender body was as exciting from the back as it was from the front, but when they got back to the house he let her shower by herself, and when at last she came nervously out into the bedroom he was gone, and she could hear faint noises from the kitchen.

She hurried into clothes, shorts which exposed the rounded curves of her backside, a bra top cut too low, and went over to the dressing table, looking for a comb. It was ridiculous to behave as though she was a shrinking virgin. She had spent five months as Alex's wife, sharing his bed, thrilling to the skill he had brought to their marriage bed, skill gained from experience allied to a vast natural talent. The man she had married might feel nothing more than patronising contempt for the opposite sex, but his pride insisted that any woman he honoured with his lust should find him a magnificent lover. And because he seemed to have an instinctive knowledge of the way a woman's body and mind worked, Amber was prepared to bet that there were very few of his women who hadn't been more than satisfied with his lovemaking.

So why was she shaking inside at the thought of re-learning just how good he was? If he realised how much he disturbed her he would enjoy stepping up the heat, playing this game of arrogant cat and angry mouse until she was sick with nerves and too strung up to be able to hide from him exactly how she reacted.

Perhaps that was what he wanted. It would be his devious way to coax her into falling in love with him again so that this time he could be the one who did the rejecting. She ran the comb through the thick clustering curls, avoiding her eyes uneasily as though she might see something embarrassing lurking in their golden depths.

Alex had made coffee and was sitting at the table eating toast and honey and watching the yacht through the kitchen window. He wore shorts, faded and tight, and a T-shirt which hid very little of the classically moulded musculature of his body. A strange little clutch of sensation deep in the pit of her stomach made Amber angry and defensive.

He stood up as she came over to the table and something deep and dangerous gleamed in his eyes, but all he said was, 'This is superb honey. How on earth do you say the name of it?'

Obligingly she told him. 'Po-hu-tu-ka-wa. Maori has the same vowel sounds as Italian, and each one is pronounced separately, so however long the word, all you have to do is break it into syllables, and the pronunciation is simple.'

'Unlike Greek,' he said mockingly, recalling her attempts to learn that language.

And that brought back memories. For one, his father's insistence and his agreement that no one address her in English or respond if she spoke English to them. Oh, even then she had known that it is much easier and quicker to learn a language that way, but it still seemed cruel to force a homesick girl into the virtual isolation which the order had caused.

But now was no time to recall that. 'Unlike Greek,' she said neutrally as he sat her in the chair opposite his. The table was small, so she had to tuck her legs beneath her chair to avoid touching his, and she kept her eyes lowered as she reached for the toast.

'You were actually becoming quite good at it,' he observed, apparently not at all embarrassed by memories of her anger and despair. 'Had you stayed you would have been speaking it like a native now.'

'As well as Gabrielle?' she asked sweetly.

He pushed a coffee cup her way. 'Fill this, please. And no, Gabrielle has never become more than able to make herself understood in the language. But then Gabrielle is French, with a Frenchwoman's lack of respect for any other language but her own. She does not speak English very well either.'

'Which is why you make love in French,' retorted Amber smoothly. 'As for speaking English, she doesn't do too badly. I understood exactly what she was saying.'

His head lifted sharply. 'What is that? You never met her.'

Amber finished pouring his refill and then poured herself a cup, waiting until she had put the pot down before answering on a dry note, 'Oh yes, I did. She came up to me as I was walking around Iraklion one day, beside the fountain, and told me that she was pregnant, and that she was glad because it meant that your first child would be hers. She pointed out that Greeks love their children, even those born the wrong side of the blanket, and that she and the baby were going to be around for all time. She smiled very sweetly at me and made it quite obvious that she didn't think I or the children I might bear were going to give her any competition.'

She looked up into eyes as clear and as hard as quartz and finished, 'You must remember that day. It was the one when I asked you in my halting Greek whether she was your mistress and you told me that she was. Then, in English, I asked you if you were going to give her up, and you told me—this time, thank goodness, in English too, or I might not have understood—that no, you weren't. Then,' she concluded thoughtfully, 'I believe I had a tantrum.'

Alex asked in an arrested voice, 'Why did you not tell me what she had said?'

She shrugged. 'It didn't really seem to matter. You'd made it quite clear where your affections lay. That was all I wanted to know.'

'My affections!' he returned harshly, and then, after a

stretched moment, 'Yes, I suppose affection is the right word. She was a clever, experienced woman, and I grew to become fond of her. The baby was a mistake, but I could not throw her out.'

'Not if you loved her, no.'

He looked at her, his narrowed glance resting with irritation on the toffee-coloured curls as she bent her head to ease her dry throat with some coffee.

'I hesitate to further blacken my character,' he said cynically, 'but I did not love her. And before you revile me further, she knew it, she had always known it. Gabrielle was—lazy, I suppose. For all her intelligence, she had no drive, no ambition. She capitalised on her looks and her skills as a lover to earn her living the easiest way she could. As a mistress she was perfect, but she did not have the stamina for a wife. A wife is linen, Gabrielle and those like her silk; both materials have their own beauty, but linen lasts for ever. Gabrielle was strictly for the good times. I always knew that if I had lost the money which kept her in luxury she would have wept a little, but she would have left me.'

He drained the coffee Amber had poured him and said coldly, 'I had not credited her with so much spite. She saw you as a threat and she worked very cleverly to nullify you. Did she tell you that I was in love with her?'

Slowly she shook her head. 'No, although I certainly got that impression.'

It seemed to be the answer he was expecting. 'She was astute enough to convince someone as lacking in confidence as you. She merely wanted to make sure that her pleasant idle life went on with no interruption. She was not grief-stricken when the child was born dead.'

Alex smiled derisively, but it was clear that the emotion was directed at himself. 'Perhaps it was fated,' he said, the oblique words falling into the tension between them, and got up as though he had made up his mind about something.

He went down below and occupied himself with whatever it was that tycoons did while Amber put the dishes into the dishwasher and ran a broom around the pristine floors. It was not yet mid-morning when she finished what few chores there were, and she was restless, her mind tired from going over and over the exchange at breakfast time.

She could remember Gabrielle Patoux as clearly as if she was still in front of her, her long Egyptian eyes amused and faintly pitying while she had done her best to ruin Amber's life. Now, after all these years, Amber found herself accepting with her heart what her mind had long been convinced of: that the Frenchwoman was as much a victim of Alex's chauvinism as she was.

Perhaps, in her own way, she loved Alex. She had felt enough for him to leave the milieu where she must have shone, the playgrounds of the rich and famous, to live on Crete near him. And it certainly indicated some form of love to deliberately have a man's child.

Amber walked out into the sun and decided to explore, setting off down a barely marked pathway through the tall scrub. It was still and quiet and very hot out of the path of the coastal breeze, and although nothing moved, the air seemed electric with small forms of life. Occasionally a grasshopper leapt away in startled agitation, and once she moved a slow stick insect from a branch at eye-level and deposited it carefully in a safer place.

Although the island was small, it was quite steep, and she was puffing when she finally got to the next point. There the trees and coastal scrub had drawn back a little from the coast so that she walked across wiry danthonia, the native grass, to come gratefully to rest against the swooping bough of another pohutukawa. The cliff was only about twenty feet high, and not very steep down to the sandy beach, the rocky slope covered with the pink flowers of convolvulus between bushes of Jerusalem apples, thorny and poisonous and tough.

Amber looked into rock pools, transparent and green, with shoals of tiny fish like silver dashes in the water; in one, slightly larger, a shadow revealed a bigger fish hanging motionless beside a rock. The warm wind barely cooled her hot cheeks. Behind her the house seemed to float against its background of bush and sea. In spite of the time and effort it had taken her to reach the point she had not left her prison far behind.

She looked out to sea with something like desperation; she could resist Alex, but only as long as he tried to intimidate her. When he dropped his guard as he had that morning at breakfast, allowing his pain at the death of his child to show in his voice and darken the depths of his eyes, she found herself opening to him like a flower. Then he was deadly dangerous.

She could, she thought wistfully, learn to like that Alex.

And that way lay perils undreamed of; as she had walked through the sizzling silence of the manuka scrub she had found herself wondering how he would react if he discovered that Nick was his son. With delight, of course, but it would be delight shot through with the fierce possessiveness she dreaded. And he would take Nick away. She could bear even that, she thought, even as her heart clutched in her throat, but she could not bear for Nick to grow up as bereft as Alex was, never knowing just how good love could be because in his heart he was convinced that women were an inferior species.

A fantail flew in its flirting, darting manner down from the bush, cheeping imperatively as it swooped on insects she had disturbed. Smiling, Amber watched it. The fan-shaped tail twisted dexterously as the tiny plump bird made incredible turns and twists in the air, its bright little eyes fixed on prey too small for Amber to see.

A call from the house sent the little hunter back to the bush and twisted her head around. Alex was standing on

the wide deck. From this distance she could almost feel
the anger emanating from him. She did not answer; he
could see her, and if he wanted her he could come to her,
she was not running back like a whipped puppy.

So she stayed still in the shade while he followed the
narrow, almost imperceptible path to where she waited.
The fantail came back, busy as ever, and she watched it
with the same faint smile. After that first yell Alex was
totally silent, moving through the thick scented manuka
scrub with as few sounds as a stalking tiger. Sun gleamed
in streaks of red on his hair as he emerged; he looked
quizzically at her, but said nothing as he came over and
sat down beside her.

'I thought you might have been foolish enough to see if
you could escape,' he said.

She shook her head, and he smiled, not very nicely.
'Oh, I realised almost immediately that I was the foolish
one. You would not run from me because that would put
your lover in a very invidious position. What he has
done to create such loyalty?'

Amber said nothing, listening to the soft tones of
danger with a rapidly beating heart. The fantail had
flown to a safe distance, but their stillness encouraged it
back.

Alex's eyes followed it. After long strained minutes he
asked, 'What is it?'

She told him. 'It's a native to Australia too. There are
two sorts, pied and black, but they mate together.'

A sweet plaintive little song came from behind them, a
series of piping notes up and down in quartertones.
Amber turned her head to look out over the sea, her eyes
crinkling as she squinted against the light.

'The bird is in the trees,' Alex observed, 'but you look
out to sea. Why is that?'

She smiled. 'That's the riroriro, the little grey warbler.
Local legend has it that it foretells rain. I was checking
the sky to see if it was imminent.'

He followed her eyes, scanning the vivid sky with a sapient regard. 'It does not look like rain to me. Do I defer to the riroriro's better knowledge of the locality?'

Amber grinned, liking him very much. 'Well, I don't know that its prediciton rate has ever been scientifically verified, but I always give or take a day. And except in drought years, rain is never very far off up here.' She pointed to the south-west, above the line of hills etched in carbon-paper blue. 'See those clouds there, those huge big shaving cream affairs? Those are summer clouds. Now those long wisps of cloud stretching down from the north quite often come with a mackerel sky, and they can mean a blow from the north. Matt is much better——' Too late she remembered Alex's prohibition. She might have made less of a hash of it if she hadn't stopped guiltily, colour seeping from her cheeks as he turned his head and she met glittering eyes which noted her stumbling effort to remain calm with cold amusement.

'You are learning,' he said after a long moment of strain, 'but I find I do not want to leave his name on that delectable mouth. Say mine.'

Her lips firmed, but she obeyed.

'Again,' he commanded softly, 'and this time put some feeling into it.'

She left him in no doubt of her feelings, spitting his name at him as though it was an obscenity.

The warning glitter faded from his eyes to be replaced by enjoyment, pure and not in the least simple. 'I think I prefer it said like that,' he said lightly. 'It pleases me to know that you dislike me and yet I can kiss you and all the dislike and suspicion are nothing against the fact that you want me.'

'I can understand that it would preen your ego,' she returned scornfully. 'But it isn't you, you know. Any presentable man would do. It's known as lust, and it's what keeps the species going.'

He grinned, mischief dancing in his eyes. 'I like it

when you are so earthy and blunt, while colour comes
and goes in your cheeks and your eyes watch me to see
how I react. You look like a deer, shy but determined,
wondering how you can get out of my trap.'

Amber shrugged, a little annoyed at the simile. 'Deer,'
she told him crisply, 'are wild and almost impossible to
handle except in a darkened room.'

And stopped, the blush rocketing up through her
skin as he threw back his head and laughed, a deep
full-throated sound of sheer enjoyment. 'Appropriate,
definitely, and before you ask, no, I did not know that
deer need to be handled in the dark. I have had little
to do with farming, although I can still milk a goat.
Tell me what you do on this farm you make your home.'

She shrugged, choosing her words with care. 'There
are actually five farms, all run as separate units—beef
and sheep, a red deer unit, Angora goats and Saanen
milking goats and a Santa Gertrudis stud. What I do is
keep track of them all. If M— if anyone wants to know
which goat in the Saanen stud produced the most milk
last year I can find out. Also, I do the wages and the
books. It keeps me busy enough.'

He nodded. 'Yes, I can see that it would. Do you enjoy
it?'

Amber looked at him suspiciously, but he seemed
straightforward. After a moment she said reluctantly,
'Yes. I feel as though I'm doing something worthwhile. I
don't get bored.'

'But it is not necessary that you do it.'

'It's necessary that someone does it,' she said stubbornly. 'If we're going to talk about necessary—how
necessary is what you do?'

'About as necessary as your work,' he said calmly. 'In
our world, someone has to produce the goods and then
distribute them, develop the economies of various
countries, help in whatever way one can the poor and
hungry.'

She was curious. In all the years she had never thought of him seeing his empire as anything but a means to power. Now she had to look at him a different way, and she was not sure that she liked it. But curiosity impelled her to ask, 'Is that how you see it?'

'Why not? A thousand years ago I could have carved out a principality for myself and kept as safe as possible those who owed me loyalty. Five hundred years ago there were new continents to discover. Now the world is old and tired, but there are many of her children who go hungry to bed each night and die of diseases which have not been seen in the West for centuries. If there were no ships to distribute produce, many more would die, many more starve. Is it so small a thing to provide the ships and the oil to run them, to support the technology which in time will give these people a better life?'

'But always at a profit.'

The words came out in a snap, but Alex didn't seem upset. He stretched lazily and lay back on the carpet of grass, admitting cheerfully, 'Altruism goes only so far, Amber. And it is not the money which gives me energy and pleasure, it is the challenges, the battles and counter-attacks. Man is a fighting animal. Now be quiet, I wish to sleep.'

Amber went to scramble up, but was stopped by strong fingers about her wrist. 'Stay with me,' he ordered softly, watching the mutiny in her expression from hooded eyes.

Her generous mouth was pinched at the corners, but she obeyed, expecting him to release her. He did, but only after his lashes had lowered in sleep, and even then the slack fingers lay curled about her wrist as though he didn't want to be separated from her.

She remembered this ability to catnap. He never suffered from jetlag because he could sleep anywhere, any time, and wake refreshed. Like Churchill, she thought, as the fantail dived perilously close. Her lashes drooped as she surveyed the handsome face, relaxed in sleep yet still controlled and dynamic. The years had dealt kindly with him. No grey touched the black hair, and the lines on his face seemed little deeper than they had nine years ago when he had been twenty-one. Yet he did not look boyish; the contours of his face spoke of maturity and power and pride.

What differences had he noticed in her? Carefully she pulled her hand free of his loose grip and rested her chin on her knees, watching him with eyes which were wistful and faintly sad. Not many, probably. Her face had slimmed down, and, courtesy of one pregnancy, her waist was not quite as narrow as it had been. Her breasts were a little bigger. It was no young girl's face which looked at her each morning from the mirror; she too bore the indefinable stamp of maturity.

Her mind roved over his description of his work. She would never have imagined that he saw his career like that. But then she hadn't really known the man she married at all, had never even tried to fathom the complexities of his mind. And he was a complex man. Clever and sophisticated, yet tied to the starkly primitive ethos of his ancestry which impelled him to carry out this mad scheme of revenge.

She should be frightened. Why then was she sitting here in the hot thrumming air of a summer's day watching him and feeling unaccountably happy?

He slept for half an hour, moving restlessly as he always had but waking to instant alertness, his eyes opening with no veil of sleep to hide their crystalline clarity.'

'Tired?' she asked inanely.

He smiled. 'Not now. It's some years since I slept under a tree with a beautiful woman beside me, however.'

Amber smiled too, allowing a touch of mockery to colour it. 'When I knew you sleeping would have been far from your mind! Growing jaded, Alex?'

His gaze sharpened. 'Is that an invitation?'

'No,' she said hastily, chagrined because deep inside she had the awful feeling that it had been. To hide her uncertainty she went on quickly, 'Why don't you let me go, Alex? You don't really want me——'

It was a mistake, she knew it was a mistake as soon as the words left her lips, but she couldn't take them back and she had to sit there cursing herself as that taunting smile slashed his face and his face grew hard and knowing.

'Sorry, darling,' he said softly, raking her with his eyes, 'have I been neglecting you, pretty thing?'

She shook her head in silent negation, but he used his strength to lever her across his knees, holding her in to the leashed power of his body with unsparing hands.

'You should have said,' he murmured, his eyes very hard and bright as they swept her shuttered face. 'All you had to do was ask, my lovely girl, and I would have been glad to oblige. I was just giving you time to get used to me again.'

He was lying, she knew that he was teasing her, tormenting her with the uncomfortable fact that her body still responded to the lure of his sexuality in subtle ways he understood, ways that his years of making love to an assortment of women had made him only too experienced in.

Like now, when the buds of breasts stiffened and became tender and sensitive, and small beads of sweat formed at her temples and across her upper lip. She felt the pangs in her breasts and the pit of her stomach, and when the leg between hers moved in a quick suggestive movement her hips rotated and her leg muscles tightened and a burning, scintillating heat sprang into full-bodied life between her thighs.

She caught her breath but managed to say curtly, 'I'm just sick and tired of waiting, that's all. If you're going to leap on me it might as well be now as later.'

Alex's brows rose at her studied vulgarity, but the face beneath her didn't tighten in disgust, and although he altered the placing of his hands, it was to pull her head down, not to push her away.

'Leap on you?' he asked in mock astonishment. 'Amber *mou*, if that is what you want, then that of course is what I'll do. But why not try it my way first? I think I can promise a little more subtlety than that.'

She opened her mouth to protest, but the words were dammed in the back of her throat as the hands behind her neck forced her head down the last few inches. His kiss was invasive and totally without tenderness, as lacking in the subtlety he had taunted her with as the hard thrust of his tongue into the depths of her mouth. Amber stiffened, but he was totally without mercy, and although she knew several ways of disabling a man she couldn't bring herself to use any of them on him.

She had no time to wonder why. In one swift smooth motion Alex reversed their positions, using his forearms to hold her still while he surveyed her furious face and swollen lips with an impassive expression.

'Apparently you like a little force,' he mused, his mouth twisting. 'Is that what you missed in my bed? I treated you like spun sugar, like the child I thought you, always careful not to hurt you, not to frighten you, and then you ran to another man. What is he like, Amber? Does he enjoy inflicting pain——?'

'Stop it,' she whispered, appalled at the ugly words and even uglier tone they were delivered in. 'Alex, it wasn't like that.'

Again those brows lifted in derisive query. 'No? But you do like things to be a little more energetic now, of course. You have much more experience. You are a woman who knows what she wants, is even able to ask for it. Let me see if I can give it to you.'

His hand smoothed down her throat; for a moment he rested one light fingertip against the pulsing hollow at the base, his narrowed eyes keenly assessing her reaction. She bit her lip, then winced at the small betrayal as something gleamed beneath his lashes. She knew what he was doing; she had seen him watch a man who was bargaining with him in just that way, searching out weak points, using body language and the hidden subliminal signals of his opponent to beat him. Then he had won himself a shipping line; this time he wanted to humiliate a woman, but he carried to both occasions that pursuit of power which sharpened his intelligence to a brilliance she feared.

'Yes, you respond so well to my hands,' he murmured, and bent his head to kiss the place where his finger had rested.

Amber fought the urgings of her body with a desperation which held her rigid and unresponsive beneath him. He wanted her aching, on fire for him, and he was going to choose the moment when he took her, not be overwhelmed by passion but with a cool assessment of the time when she would be most humiliated. His character demanded that he dominate and he would use her sexuality to shame her and reinforce his own image of himself.

It seemed such an incredible waste. Amber lay quiescent as his mouth tasted the fine contours of her throat, the hollows, the sensitive spot where her neck joined her shoulder. Was he afraid of giving himself into another's keeping? Her eyes opened, slitted against the sun, and she wondered if beneath that sleek self-possessed exterior there was a pit of insecurity, hidden yet recognised at subconscious level by the man who had everything.

Her dreaming eyes followed the fantail. All conscious thought was submerged by a tide of pleasure so intense that she groaned with it, the sound thick on the sparkling air. Alex smiled against her breast and his mouth tugged sweetly, painfully, suckling with such erotic enjoyment that she went up in flames. The hand that touched the dark fire of his hair was shaking; she whispered his name as she threaded her fingers through the warm silk, holding him against her.

His hand slid the length of her ribcage, the fingertips kindling small points of fire on her skin before moving to the slender length of her leg. He said, 'So smooth and sleek, like silk over steel . . .' and a shudder rippled through her body at the sensuous sweep of his palm up her thigh.

The little bra top lay discarded beneath her; she felt his fingers at the ties which held the shorts together at the side, and although she wanted to protest at his invasion the words would not form on her slack lips, and she had to suffer the realisation that all that she wore was a tiny scrap of lace and silk chosen by him for just such an occasion.

As he had chosen the top, with its front fastening, and the scanty little shorts.

She muttered, 'Don't,' but her heart wasn't in it, and when his fingers slid beneath the lace and silk she convulsed, shamefully, his name torn from her lips in an agony of desire.

CHAPTER SIX

'YOU want me,' whispered Alex in the rough voice of one who had little control over his vocal chords.

'Yes.' It was stupid to say no; that devilish hand twisted, applied pressure, and again Amber was racked by an intolerable need.

'Say it,' he insisted, half beneath his breath.

'Alex . . .' Her voice trailed away as he moved his head far enough to accommodate the other nipple. 'Say it,' he demanded after long moments when the drawing of his mouth was a sweet agony forging fiery paths through her body. 'Tell me that you want me, Amber *mou*.'

She said it, unable to prevent herself, but he was not satisfied. 'Again!'

Torn in two by desire, she would have done anything, said anything to persuade him to satisfy her unbearable desire.

'I want you,' she said, 'please—oh, please, Alex . . .'

His hand, his mouth stopped. For a long time he lay dragging breath into his lungs, and then he sat up and looked down into her dazed, avid face, and said deliberately, 'Of course you do. Infuriating, isn't it, to want the man you despise so? Come, let us go on. I have a desire to circumnavigate our little prison.'

Amber had expected something like this, braced herself for it, but even so her body throbbed with unsatisfied hunger and she could have killed him for his cynical exploitation of her needs. He watched as her fingers curled, watched as she carefully relaxed them, the same sardonic little smile pulling at the corners of his mouth, and when he looked into her face it was with eyes from which the last shred of passion had fled, leaving

111

them as cold and as welcoming as a Polar sea.

Numbly she tied the ridiculous little ties on her shorts, and pulled the bra top around her body. Before she had a chance to fasten it he stooped and pulled her to her feet, plucking the material from her fingers.

'I think I prefer you to go without that,' he said calmly as he hung it over a twig.

She didn't plead with him, although she could feel the blush over her exposed breasts. Instead she took the scrap of material and stuffed it into the pocket in his shirt.

'I'd just as soon not be seen by any passing yachtsman like this,' she said levelly.

Alex shot her an ironic look. 'No yachtsman will get close enough to see you.'

She shrugged, 'They can land and walk along the beach up to high-water mark, and most will see nothing wrong in exploring the island if they don't leave any trace of their presence. There are also such things as binoculars.'

'I have riparian rights,' he told her succinctly, 'which I certainly intend to enforce, and if any yacht comes too near then we will retire into the trees. Come.'

But he left the bra in his pocket.

Head held so high that her neck ached, Amber preceded him down the narrow path. Strangely, and he would probably be intensely irritated if he knew it, she didn't feel embarrassed. The island was like Eden, still and quiet and with a vibrant waiting quality which kept her alert and vaguely excited. And once the claw of passion had been eased by exertion she found she was enjoying herself.

Much of that was due to Alex. He didn't treat her with the crude sexism she half expected; certainly his eyes admired the gentle curves of her breasts, but it was an aesthetic admiration spiced only a little by desire. She felt appreciated, beautiful as Eve.

He wore a pair of shorts, faded and old, which clung lovingly to his lean flanks, and above them a sleeveless black tee-shirt, the knitted material revealing every movement of every muscle in his torso. Like Amber he was barefooted, but he moved with the easy grace of a man wholly at home with his surroundings.

Amber had to drag her eyes away from him and swallow to ease a suddenly dry mouth. He was sinfully attractive, and she should not be allowing this rising tide of pleasure to blind her to his other attributes, the dangerous arrogance and the harsh code he lived by.

The island was rougher around the seaward side, the cliffs a little higher and steeper, the scrub turning into trees which were bent by fiercer winds from the ocean, but it was fairly easy going until they came down into a gully where the manuka bushes grew tall and dense, the wiry branches with their needle leaves crowding in on the track.

'I'll go first,' said Alex, automatically holding back branches for her.

Amber slid through them, avoiding the scratchy twigs. One landed on her shoulder and she brushed at it, then brushed at it again. It wasn't until she felt it move that she realised what it was, and when the beleaguered insect bit into the tender flesh she could only grunt with shock and make a wild dab at it.

Alex exclaimed something and was by her side in an instant, knocking the weta to the ground and holding her in his warm grip, demanding urgently, 'What the hell was that? Is it poisonous? It bit you—see, there is blood!'

Relief shook her knees. She babbled, 'No, oh no, it was just a weta, a native cricket. It's all right. Normally they don't bite, but I frightened it when I tried to knock it off, poor thing. I'm not really frightened of them, although they look a bit fierce——'

'Hush,' he said gently, and she rested her head in the hollow of his shoulder and stood quietly listening to his

heart. He moved a little and his mouth came down where
the insect had bitten. Amber held her breath as his
tongue touched the small bead of blood. They stood
frozen in the summer air as he removed the small
effusion, then slid his mouth across the tender skin in a
kiss as comforting as it was sexually exciting.

What sort of man was he? A man who inflicted
humiliation with a careless disdain, then didn't carry it
through. A man who held a woman in the safe cradle of
his arms after refusing the offer of her body. I don't know
you, she thought, and for some idiotic reason tears came
to her eyes. She blinked them down, sniffing inelegantly,
and his chest lifted a little as he asked, 'Where is your
handkerchief?'

'These shorts don't have room for a handkerchief.'

She felt his chuckle, then he fished his own out and
pushed it into her hand, saying severely, 'My mother was
always very angry with me when I lost my handkerchief.
As for sniffing . . .!'

Amber mopped up and stepped free of him, holding
out the linen square with a half smile. He took it from her
and gravely held out the bra. Neither spoke. Amber
stood with the narrow band of material looped over her
hand and looked at him, wondering what he was
thinking behind that bland mask.

'Put it on,' he said calmly, 'or I might begin to think
you enjoy parading around half-naked in front of me.'

Colour flamed through her skin; to the sound of his
chuckle she turned away and with awkward movements
hurried into the top. But when she was in it and they were
walking down towards the beach something impelled her
to say, 'Actually, it was rather nice. I felt—oh, free, I
suppose.'

'Don't tell anyone,' he said instantly. 'I have interests
in the fashion business.'

She laughed, and didn't reveal that it was his attitude,
so free of sexual innuendo, which had given her the

freedom to enjoy going topless. A strange, complex man.

It was impossible to drag her hungry eyes from his body; they insisted on admiring the elegant sinuous line of movement from shoulder through to hip and down each long leg as he walked. Like a panther, she thought. Smooth and co-ordinated and supple, strength allied to beauty. It was no wonder that her whole being responded in joyful pagan hunger to him.

Alex stopped so suddenly that she almost walked into him.

'What is it?'

'Quiet!'

Almost immediately she heard what he had. Voices, all masculine, not very far ahead.

'Stay here,' he said softly as he started along the path. Frowning, Amber followed. He stopped again and turned an impatient, authoritative face to her. 'I said, stay here.'

'Why? It will just be yachties. Alex, this is New Zealand, there's no need to get uptight because you hear voices!'

'Does no one ever get mugged in New Zealand?'

She reacted to the derision in his voice with a smile. 'A few. But believe me, there's no reason to be alarmed at the sound of voices on a beach.'

'They could be reporters.'

She hadn't even thought of that. The days of avoiding reporters were long past for her. A litle worriedly she objected, 'Not New Zealand ones, the newspapers here don't work like that. And those are most definitely New Zealand accents.'

Alex nodded but didn't appear to be entirely convinced by her argument. Not that she blamed him; she knew how harried by reporters he was. They were still looking at each other when a young boy came hurtling around a tree, tripped and landed fair and square on his stomach at Alex's feet. The resounding *whomp* as his small body hit the ground stole his breath from him; he lay gasping and clawing for air until Alex picked him up and set him on his feet, one tanned arm supporting him while he fought for breath.

When it came he wriggled free, apologising, 'Gee, I'm sorry, I didn't see you. Where's your yacht?'

Alex laughed. 'I have no yacht. I live here.'

The boy, about ten or eleven, looked impressed. 'In the Yank's house? Are you the millionaire?'

'Do I sound like an American millionaire?'

He shook his head, reluctantly giving up the American. 'No, but you're foreign, aren't you?'

'Yes, I am foreign. Where were you going?'

'Just for a run.' The boy wriggled again. 'This is the first time I've been off the boat today.'

Nothing further needed to be said. Naturally he needed to let off steam. Alex advised mildly, 'You had better slow down and watch your footing, the path is narrow and uneven.'

With casual aplomb, the boy said, 'Oh, I won't go any further, I'll come back with you.'

He chatted artlessly, informing them that he was with his family and his uncle Phil, and they had hired a yacht for a week. He had caught three snapper and a kahawai, all of which they had eaten, and yesterday his father had hooked something which took off at such a rate that they decided it must have been a tuna.

'A skipjack, *I* reckon,' he said, relishing the word. Above his head Amber's eyes met Alex's in shared amusement.

He was a nice boy; his name was Brent Jones, and when Alex solemnly introduced himself and Amber he shook hands with endearing formality and invited them to the barbecue his family were planning to have on the beach.

'Dad and Uncle Phil went diving,' he confided, 'and they got some crayfish, so Mum said she'd do it in foil on the barbecue.' Something struck him and he turned alarmed blue eyes up to Alex. 'I suppose it's all right to have a barbecue on this island?'

Amber, recalling Alex's insistence on privacy, wondered what he would do. After a hesitation so slight that Brent didn't notice, he said, 'Yes, provided you do not disturb anything or set fire to the trees.'

'Not likely.' He was very endearing in his earnestness. 'We're very careful. Mum said this is almost the only island in the bay where the bush still comes down to the beach, so it's special.'

They came out of the trees and on to the sand, white and hot, of a beach which was almost opposite the cove where the house was. Amber surveyed the group of people, although not as keenly as the man beside her. But not even he could see anything to be wary of in the family party who were cheerfully setting up a portable barbecue well away from the overhanging trees.

Their arrival was noticed immediately. The woman looked up and said something to the man beside her, who put aside the basket of crayfish he was handling and came towards them.

'Dad, this is Mr Stevens and Mrs Stevens,' Brent announced proudly, doing his best with the surname. 'They own the island, but it's all right if we have a picnic. I told them we wouldn't make any mess or hurt the birds.'

His parents received them with the warm hospitality which Amber had learned was a characteristic of New Zealanders; she was not surprised at their friendliness, or the way they seconded their son's invitation, but she was startled when Alex agreed. Especially when she watched his eyes narrow as Mrs Jones introduced her brother, a pleasantly good-looking man in his early thirties whose name was Phil Waring, and who seemed to find the honey-coloured length of Amber's legs more than a little eye-catching. She was a litle embarrassed at his open appreciation, even although there was nothing unpleasant about it, but Alex bristled, keeping her beside him with a coolly possessive hand.

They had spread a large rug beneath the overhanging branches, and it was to this that Mrs Jones led them, saying, 'The barbecue is a gas one, so we don't have to wait for coals to form. Come and have a drink while the children work off some of their energy in the sea.'

Amber had to hide a small smile as she saw Alex drinking cask wine, but no one would have known by his expression that he was accustomed to only the best champagne. For her part she found it pleasantly fruity and deliciously refreshing in the hot day.

Mr Jones had been looking a little self-conscious, and only waited for them all to be served their drinks before he made the reason known. 'We do know that we shouldn't be here,' he said to Alex. 'It's marked on the chart that you have riparian rights, so we do know we're trespassing.'

Alex lifted a brow but said only, 'You don't look the sort of person who will cut down the trees or shoot the wood-pigeons.'

They all looked appalled. 'Heavens, no,' Mrs Jones said eagerly, 'that's actually why we decided to come here. It's so beautiful with the forest cover still on, we thought the children should see it.'

She flushed faintly, and Alex supplied with a hint of cynicism, 'Before the owner cuts the trees down and builds a hotel all over it.'

'Well, we can't expect someone who's not a New Zealander to understand our love for the bush. Not when we seem to have done our best over the past hundred years to denude the country of it! It's really only in the past ten or twenty years that New Zealanders have realised just how precious the few remnants are.'

Alex smiled, reducing her to servitude. 'The American who used to own the island was very concerned with conservation, and I am Greek, I understand exactly what it is like to live where the forest cover has been felled. No trees will be removed while I own the island.'

They hid their curiosity with enthusiastic approval of his stance. The conversation followed his lead, and the next twenty minutes were spent discussing the conservation movement. Amber sat without talking much, happy to listen in a state of dreamy contentment. In the sea, watched without being obvious by their parents, the Jones children frolicked, their voices a pleasant counterpoint to the shirring of the cicadas in the trees.

Summer in New Zealand, Amber thought, her golden eyes moving across the shining curve of sand to the cool sparkle of the waters and thence out to the distant thin line where the sea met a sky which throbbed brazenly around the jewel of the sun. Sails swayed and dipped like distant butterflies and the sun drew a golden mantle over sea and land alike. Purerua, the hill which formed the northern head of the deep inlet which was the Bay of Islands, was sharply defined against the sky, steep and fortresslike, with the gentler lines of the farmland on its long peninsula leading back to the mainland.

Amber sighed. She had come to love New Zealand dearly, yet in her heart there was a wistful longing for the land of her birth. The little hiss of breath through her lips had been noiseless, but when she looked up she found Phil Waring watching her. He smiled and she smiled back, thinking nothing of the small intimacy.

But beside her she felt Alex stiffen, and without missing a step he drew her into the conversation. She saw Phil look hastily away and realised what had happened. Without saying a word, Alex had warned him off. Anger gave a glittering intensity to her gaze, and when Mrs Jones said cheerfully, 'I suppose we'd better get these crayfish cooked,' Amber too got to her feet, saying above the other woman's protests that she had never cooked crayfish on a barbecue and she'd like to see how it was done.

It was pleasant to chat quietly with her hostess as the crayfish grilled. They spoke inconsequentially of the difficulties of dealing with children's appetites and other motherly things, then the children came running up, brown and sleek as seals in the sun, and after they had dried off a little their mother gave brisk orders and within a few minutes they were sitting around a feast.

Alex enjoyed it immensely, strong teeth flashing in the deeply tanned skin of his face as he tried the crayfish, and made Mrs Jones' day by pronouncing it as good as any lobster he'd eaten. The salads were crisp and cool from the insulated bin, and at the bottom were peaches and melons and nectarines and late oranges.

'We went up to Kerikeri yesterday and bought up large,' Mrs Jones told them. 'The fruit there is incredibly cheap. We found a stall which had strawberries at half the price in Auckland!'

'Must be all those orchards and market gardens,' her oldest son said teasingly, grinning at her when she pulled a face in answer.

They were a pleasant family. Sitting there drowsily in the sun, her fingers sticky with peach juice, Amber remembered other picnics with Matt and Nick, and a wave of nostalgia and homesickness and foreboding swept over her, destroying in an instant the lazy pleasure she had been feeling.

She didn't think anyone else had noticed; she lowered her head, using the peach in her hand to shield herself, but Phil Waring asked softly, 'Are you all right?'

'Yes,' she said, desperate to be discreet.

Too late. Alex's finger lifted her chin; he took one look at her face and said calmly, 'I think I'd better get you home.'

Amber hissed a denial at him, but by now everybody had noticed what was going on, and Mrs Jones began to fuss a little.

'No, it's probably a little too much sun,' said Alex,

getting to his feet. He extended a hand to Amber and, angry and still a little shaky, she allowed him to pull her up.

He made their goodbyes with perfect courtesy and a determination so obvious that no one attempted to persuade them to stay. Within five minutes they were back in the coolness of the trees, taking a short cut through the low ridge which divided the two hills on either end of the island, and Amber was protesting, 'I feel fine, I really do.'

'You are still pale,' Alex told her dismissively.

'But there was no need to break things up like that. I'm not sick.'

He shrugged. 'Perhaps not. But while you may have enjoyed being ogled by that oaf I was tired of watching him run his eyes up and down your legs. You happen to be my wife, not some cheap beach girl.'

Stung by the rank injustice, she snapped, 'If you hadn't forced me to wear clothes that make me look exactly that, there'd have been no reason for him to think that I was your mistress, and therefore free game. But he was not ogling, for heaven's sake! He seemed a nice man with an ordinary man's appreciaton of the acres of female skin I happen to be displaying, thanks to you!'

'You enjoyed it.'

The accusation brought hot blood to her cheeks. She said icily, 'Don't be so bloody ridiculous.'

Alex stopped, jerking her about to face him, and something in her heart quailed at the fierce glitter of the gaze he bent on her. 'Don't swear at me!' he snapped.

'I'll swear at you——' She stopped, struck at the stupidity of their behaviour. After a shocked moment, she looked away from him and said uncertainly, 'Alex, this is ludicrous. Why are we arguing? You know perfectly well that there was nothing in Phil Waring's expression but the normal male pleasure in a reasonably

attractive woman. You can't possibly be jealous. Or
angry.'

'Then how is it that I am both?' He let her go and
stepped back, running a hand through his hair. But the
swift aggression was fading from his face, and he said
ruefully, 'I must be losing my mind. I have never shared,
and I did not like the way he was looking at you, but you
are right, it should not have made me lose my temper.
After all,' with a bite in his tone,' at the moment I am the
man in possession.'

Which was as near to an apology as she was likely to
get. By the time they got back to the house Amber was
fully recovered, but agreed without demur to his order
that she lie down on the big bed and try to sleep while he
used the equipment in the downstairs office to earn a few
more millions.

Not that he put it like that, of course, and she was a
little ashamed of the cynical thought. As she drifted off to
sleep she thought that the picnic was her ideal of a happy
family life. If she had married someone who did not
consider he had a God-given right to look for romance
outside the marriage bed, perhaps picnics like that would
be a commonplace element in her life.

Were there many men who enjoyed family life as Ewan
Jones so patently did? Not a lot, she thought sadly,
certainly not in the circles in which Alex moved. Most of
the girls she had gone to school with had parents who
were divorced, and many of the people she had met in the
time of that brief marriage had broken marriages. The
temptations were great; it was not just Alex who was
marked down as prey. Sometimes Amber felt a vast
contempt for her own sex, thinking of the women who
used their beauty as a way to riches. But that was not fair,
there were infinitely more who stayed with men who
were hardly the stuff of dreams.

Perhaps we expect too much, she thought drowsily.
Perhaps there's no such thing as romantic love. Or if

there is, perhaps it doesn't last in the hard, clear light of everyday life.

She woke as the sun was losing itself behind a bank of clouds, and yawned and stretched, feeling a faint taste of stale wine in her mouth which prompted her into the bathroom to clean her teeth.

She had stripped to get on to the bed, and now she showered and put on a sun-frock, distaste at the extreme cut turning the corners of her mouth down, but she was unable to find anything less revealing to wear. When she came out into the sitting room she saw Alex on the deck, lying on a lounger with a book. His head turned as she came into the room and as if summoned by an invisible signal she went out to him.

He watched her come towards him and she felt a sudden wild disappointment. That morning she had hoped they had achieved a fragile peace, some sort of understanding, but there was no sign of that in the insolent appraisal that scorched the length of her body. The smile which curved his mouth was almost leering; he stayed where he was and watched as Amber sat down a distance from him.

When she was seated he said, 'Come over here.'

Angry colour beat up through her skin, but she met the flat danger of his eyes and came over to stand by the lounger.

'Sit down,' he ordered, voice bored.

She found a small space beside him and sat on it, hating the way he looked at her. After that first look he had kept his eyes on her breasts; the dress was backless and halternecked, the front opening plunging almost to her navel, held together only at the waist by a tie. She was not particularly voluptuous, but the cut was such that the soft curves of her breasts were exposed to his eyes.

A faint burr from some electronic device brought her head around; he said reluctantly, 'That is someone trying to contact me. I shouldn't be long.

He was about ten minutes, time Amber spent watching the sun gleam and beckon on the waters, emptying her mind, trying to achieve some peace. But she was still nervous when a noise brought her attention back with a jerk. She looked around, and what she saw in his face drove her to her feet, his name on her lips.

He hesitated, and she saw that for perhaps the first time in his life he didn't know what to say. Such an uncharacteristic loss of confidence frightened her; her eyes widened as she whispered. 'Alex, what—Alex! Is it Nick? It is Nick—he's been hurt! For God's sake, *tell* me!'

He was beside her in two long strides, setting firm hands on her shoulders. 'You will keep calm!' he ordered.

Amber pinned him with eyes from which all gold had fled. 'I'm all right,' she declared. 'What's happened?'

'It is your son. He has fallen over a cliff on an island and is in hospital in Auckland with head injuries.'

She caught her breath but asked steadily enough, 'How badly hurt is he?'

'He is still unconscious.'

'Has he fractured his skull? Is it concussion or is he in a coma?'

He said evenly, 'There is that possibility. According to the message your cousin's housekeeper passed on, the surgeon in charge suggests you waste no time getting there.'

Horror and an agony so intense that it almost brought her to her knees tore through her. She pressed a hand to her eyes and swayed, and instantly Alex's hands tightened and she was pulled into the warmth of his arms. He offered the simple consolation of his humanity, holding her in a passionless embrace until she straightened to say in a voice from which all emotion had been banished, 'I'll have to get ready.'

'I told my manager in Auckland to contact your housekeeper and get her to pack a suitcase for you and send it down by courier. It should reach the hotel by tonight. Kostas is already on the way in the helicopter.'

She nodded, accepting his help without surprise, concentrating only on keeping herself in one piece. Fiercely she fought down the fear that clawed at her; she would be no help to Nick if she surrendered to it. She knew enough of the normal caginess of hospital staff to understand that they had tacitly admitted that they were not happy about Nick's chances. By refusing to admit the possibility of his death perhaps she could hold it at bay— at least until she reached him.

It seemed hours before the helicopter landed, but was only a few minutes, long enough for her to pack a few clothes and go automatically tidying up around the house, locking windows and doors, cleaning out the fridge, her face set and white. Alex left her alone but was never very far away. A solemn Kostas handed her into the machine, casting her a sympathetic glance before he applied himself to getting them to the landing pad at the hospital as fast as possible.

The journey was a kaleidoscope, a phantasmagoria of awful wrenching apprehension and a fear that lay in her heart like a dead thing. She thought of nothing else but her son facing death without her, was barely conscious of Alex, grim-faced and silent, beside her.

Somewhere on the way she asked tonelessly, 'Do you know what happened?'

'I am afraid not. A man called Kyle Beringer contacted your housekeeper, but told her little more than that the boy had fallen over a cliff and that your cousin had broken a leg rescuing him. They were flown into Auckland by police helicopter. Your cousin is in a satisfactory condition and the boy is holding his own.' He covered her hands, white as her face, and held them imprisoned in his warm grasp, commanding incisively, 'You must not give up hope, Amber. He may well have recovered consciousness by the time we arrive there, and a coma is not necessarily dangerous.'

'He was so excited,' she said without expression. 'I thought he was too young to go, but Matt said I was over-protective. He promised to watch him . . .'

'No one can watch over a child every second.'

'I know,' she answered. 'I know. Especially a boy like Nick. He's such a determined kid, he's bright and brave and bold, the sort of boy who creates havoc through sheer exuberance. But never the same havoc twice.'

He must have realised how close she was to breaking point, because he turned the subject. 'Who is Kyle Beringer?'

'A friend of Matt's—he has a station north of Auckland. Did you ever know of Dan Evans? He was an Australian industrialist who died tragically young, oh, ten years or so ago.'

Alex nodded. 'Yes, I had some dealings with him just before he died. He had a very beautiful wife.'

'Trust you to notice!' said Amber with a faint attempt at a smile. 'That's Arminel. She and Dan were only married a couple of years before he died. She had his little girl, then some years after Dan died she married Kyle. They have a son, Sam.'

Her voice ran down and he prompted, 'What made them decide to go on this cruise?'

Why couldn't he leave her alone? Every cell in her brain resisted his probing, but one glance at him warned her that he was not going to let her sit alone, hounded by her fear.

In a dragging voice she replied, 'Oh, Kyle suggested it just before Christmas. At first Arminel and I were going to go too, but she decided to stay at home as she's pregnant, and I had a lot of work to catch up on after Christmas. The Angora sale is early in February and there's always a lot of organising to do. But Matt needed a holiday, so they decided to take the boys.'

Tears blurred her vision and she finished with a catch

in her voice. She was grateful that Alex did not patronise her with empty comfort, grateful too for the warm security of his hand around hers.

Without looking at him she leaned her head back on the seat and tried to empty her mind of the panic which made such a mess of her thought processes. Deep breathing helped. At least it gave her something to concentrate on other than hideous visions of Nick hurt and in pain.

At last Kostas brought the helicopter down with a flourish and assisted Amber out, his handsome face expressing warm concern. She gave him a small smile of thanks before drawing a last deep breath, then turned, her eyes stark with apprehension as Alex took her arm and accompanied her across to the small deputation who waited out of range of the rotors. Amber recognised only Kyle Beringer, a couple of inches taller than anyone else and with the face of a dark angel; the rest of the group were strangers.

'Kyle,' she said imploringly, half beneath her breath.

His eyes flicked from her to fix for a desperate second on Alex. She saw swift comprehension in them and could not prevent naked fear from showing in her face. Immediately Kyle's expression settled back into an impassive mask. He took her hands and held them tight, reaching down to kiss her cheek.

'He's not yet conscious,' he said crisply, 'but he's holding his own.'

She gave a little half sob of relief and said unevenly, 'Kyle, this is Alex Stephanides. He—that is——'

'I am Amber's husband,' Alex's voice was neutral, even a little bored, but she noticed the swift appraisal he gave Kyle as they shook hands.

Kyle introduced the surgeon who was in charge of Nick's case and another man who turned out to be the representative of the Stephanides Corporation in Auckland; it was he who had telephoned the message through to the island. He was clearly more than curious, and equally clearly determined not to show it.

Amber forced herself to go through the ritual of greeting while her whole being screamed urgency, her demand to be with Nick written so expressively in the pinched pallor of her face that the surgeon said quietly, 'If you would come with me, Mr and Mrs Stephanides, I'll take you to your son. And please believe that we're doing all that we can.'

'And how much is that?'

It was Alex who asked; the doctor's misapprehension had sealed Amber's tongue to the roof of her mouth. She stole a look at Alex, to see if he was going to repudiate Nick as his son, but he was still watching the surgeon with hard authority as though if necessary he would crack the other man's skull to get at the truth.

'As much as any hospital in the world,' the doctor said, calmly unintimidated as he led the way into the hospital.

Amber asked, 'How bad are his injuries?'

The doctor flashed her a quick glance, testing her mettle, she supposed. Whatever he saw apparently satisfied him, because he explained, 'It's difficult to say with head injuries. The X-rays show no sign of any fracture to the skull, but the unconsciousness is not a good sign, although not necessarily a bad one, either. We are monitoring him carefully, but at the moment all that I can confidently say is that he is in a coma and in a stable condition. You have no reason to fear the worst.'

Alex took Amber's elbow, his fingers conveying support. All he said, however, was a crisp thanks.

They walked quickly through what seemed endless corridors, but it didn't take long for them to arrive at the room where Nick lay, small and chalk-white in the hospital bed, his long dark lashes sweeping across cheeks which had lost their childhood plumpness to reveal the stark bone structure of the man he would grow to be. Amber realised with a shock that in maturity he would look very like his father. If he reached maturity.

In a voice she didn't recognise as her own she asked, 'Did he sustain any other injuries?'

'No, he was lucky. There are a few bruises, but that's all. I understand that his uncle protected him with his own body.'

Amber fought down another sob. She moved across to take the small hand, still slightly grubby, and stated in tones which rang around the quiet room, 'He's going to get better. Starting now.' Her eyes swept around the faces of the men, then dropped to that of her son.

It was a confident challenge flung at fate, but as she waited the long hours away beside his bed she began to wonder if it had been too confident. Although Nick held his own, he didn't show any signs of emerging from the insidious amnesia of unconsciousness, and Amber knew enough to realise that each hour he spent in the twilight world which held him fast made it more difficult for him to escape.

All that day she stayed with him, talking to his unresponsive form, unable to leave him. Some time just before the sun set Alex came back and stood over her while she picked at a meal his hotel had sent along; when she pushed the tray away he said crisply, 'I believe your cousin wishes to see you.'

She stared at him, breathing in horrified tones, 'I'd completely forgotten about him!'

Impassively he said, 'He has been asking for you.'

'I'll have to see him.' But her eyes betrayed her reluctance to leave Nick.

'Do you wish me to stay with the boy?'

She said in a stifled voice, 'I can't ask you to——'

'You have not asked, I have offered. Now go.'

Amber cast a last look at the still figure in the bed. She said, 'Alex, you've been very kind—I don't want you to feel obliged to stay——'

Embarrassment as well as strain made her tones faint.

He listened courteously until her voice faded away, then said without intonation, 'I have business to do in Auckland. I shall stay until things are settled, I think.' And when she would have protested he smiled, an unpleasant, derisive smile with the mockery directed in equal parts to himself and her, and finished, 'Think of it as a humanitarian impulse, Amber. I have so few that it would be a pity to rob me of the chance to indulge in one.'

I'll never understand him, she thought as she left the ward. Never, never, never.

Matt was on a different floor, lying with his leg in traction, his handsome face drawn. He looked at her with opaque eyes and she realised with consternation and horror that he was braced for her to blame him.

'Oh, Matt,' she stammered as she came up to his bed, holding hard on to her voice so that it didn't tremble. She leaned down and kissed his cheek, hugging his head to her breast. 'Matt, I should have come to see you earlier, but I'm so sorry, I couldn't think beyond Nick. Please forgive me.'

'Forgive you?' His heavy tone told her how much he reproached himself. 'God, Amber, I'm the one who should beg forgiveness! I told you I'd make sure nothing happened to him!'

She tightened her arm, looking at the harsh line of his profile against her breast, and said gently, 'You're not to blame yourself! I know—who better?—that it's just not possible to keep track of Nick every minute of every day. What happened?'

'Kyle didn't tell you?'

She said carefully, 'I didn't see him for very long, he had to leave almost as soon as we arrived. I'm afraid I was too busy asking the neuro-surgeon what was wrong to talk much to Kyle.'

'Yes, he called in to see me just before you got here. He had to go—Arminel isn't very well and their doctor wants him at home.' He pulled away from her, settling himself back against the pillows. Only his sudden pallor revealed that he was in pain. Wearily he went on, 'It happened just after we'd gone ashore; Nick and I were following Kyle and Sam along a path at the top of a cliff and without any warning it fell away beneath our feet. I tried—Amber, I swear I did my best to shield him, but he was torn out of my arms. I got hit by a rock and knocked out. When I came to we were both in the helicopter being ferried back here. How is he? They've given me nothing but soothing platitudes.'

When she told him how she had left Nick his eyes closed, but almost immediately they opened and he said confidently, 'He's a tough little character; if anyone's going to make it he will.'

Another man who didn't believe in the comforting falsehood. Unable to speak, Amber nodded and he went on, 'I know you want to be with him, so off you go. If you can, keep me posted, will you?'

'Of course I will.' Indecision drew her to gnaw a moment on her lip before deciding on the direct approach. 'Alex is here—Alex Stephanides.'

'What?' Matt went grey with shock.

She nodded and hurried on, 'Apparently he never stopped looking for me, and when your name and the fact that you were my father's only living relative turned up in my father's papers, he decided it was worth tracking you down. He was my father's executor, you see. My father left him everything.'

Matt put out a hand and caught her wrist. In spite of the events of the day his grip was imperative. 'What does he want?' he demanded raggedly. 'Tell me!'

Amber shrugged, trying to infuse her voice with lightness. 'He thinks—I let him think that you and I are living in sin and that Nick is yours.'

Matt drew his breath in on a silent whistle. His fingers bit into her wrist, but relaxed at her unguarded movement. 'I see,' he said slowly, and she knew that he did.

After a moment he said, 'I'll back you up, of course. But, Amber, why is he so certain Nick isn't his?'

She told him, blushing a little even now, finishing, 'I suppose he thought it was a dream. Well, until I found I was pregnant, I was convinced I'd dreamed the incident. Oh God, Matt, I just wish I hadn't got you mixed up with it!'

'What was he doing when—why did he come with you? Surely he must realise that you're under enough stress without him adding to it? Is he totally insensitive?'

Amber lied flatly and without hesitation. 'I doubt if he'll stay long. He has a great sense of responsibility. It simply wouldn't occur to him to leave me without someone to look after me. He's going to get a divorce when he goes back.' She even managed a smile as a nurse came towards them.

She could see that Matt didn't know whether to believe her or not, but the providential arrival of the nurse put an end to the conversation. Amber hastily kissed him and left him to the ministrations of the woman, who was young and clearly interested in her handsome patient, and hurried back to Nick.

CHAPTER SEVEN

NEVER before had Amber known what it was to be cold. Fear she knew, but not this icy panic which ate its way into her bones, holding her imprisoned in a cell where no one could reach her to warm her. Nick lay like a small pale wraith, his face shuttered and quiet as though the keen quick mind had gone somewhere else and she was sitting beside the shell of her son. As she sang to him and talked to him and read from his favourite books, made up silly jokes and riddles, each hour that went past made it harder for her to keep her voice light and confident.

And each day when she went to see Matt she saw her own dread hidden in his eyes.

She recognised only the doctor and Matt and Alex. How Alex spent the time while she fought her battle by Nick's bed she had no idea, but he came to the hospital twice each day, and it was he, after a suggestion made by one of the nurses, who organised the delivery of a selection of children's books from one of the bookshops in town. Amber was grateful to him for the impersonal kindness he was showing, but was unable to respond. All her energy was being used in the fight for her son.

Once, early in the second day, she suggested that he must have business to see to elsewhere and noticed with an abstract interest that his expression darkened. On an unusually crisp note he told her he thought he was more needed here, and when she stared at him with blank eyes he gave a wolfish smile and said, 'There are plenty of pickings, Amber. The Corporation has interests in New Zealand. It is not doing them any harm to receive a visit from me.'

So she nodded and went back into the silent ward, and

if she thought of Alex it was with a distant wonder, as
though he was a being from another planet.

Until, after a long night of strain, the doctor
exchanged a look with Alex and said, 'Mrs Stephanides,
if you don't get some rest we'll have to treat you for
exhaustion. You must sleep.'

'He might need me.'

Patiently, he said, 'If he does you'll be rung. Your
husband tells me there's a suite for you at the hotel only a
few hundred yards away. I strongly suggest that you go
there and get some rest. Exhausted, you're no use to
anyone.'

Amber met his adamant gaze and admitted reluctantly
that he was right. She was so weary that she couldn't even
see straight, yet it was incredibly difficult to leave Nick;
she gave him a piteous glance and kissed the smooth pale
brow before she was urged away by Alex's impersonal
hand on her elbow.

At the hotel they were greeted with all the deference
that the name Stephanides gave rise to, and for once it
was welcome; it meant that she didn't even have to
think. In the silent air-conditioned comfort of the suite
she showered, then fell naked into bed and slept, and
woke to afternoon and the sound of someone moving
around in the sitting room.

'Who is it?' she called uncertainly.

Alex appeared in the doorway, shirtsleeves rolled up,
his expression tightly controlled.

'What are you doing here?' Conscious that she wore
nothing beneath the thin percale sheet, Amber clutched
it betrayingly as colour touched her pale cheeks.

'Working,' he told her indifferently.

Her face was split with a yawn; when it was possible to
speak again she asked, 'What time is it?'

'Almost one o'clock in the afternoon. You have slept
too few hours. I will send for lunch.' He frowned at the
quick shake of her head and insisted firmly, 'You have

lost weight. Starving yourself is not going to help your son get better.'

Your son, he said, and did not know that Nick was his son too. For the first time Amber wondered if she had had any right to make the decision that separated Nick from his father. Shaken by another yawn, she pushed the uncomfortable query to the back of her mind and had to firm her mouth to say, 'Oh, very well. I need a shower first, though.'

The food was waiting when she emerged from the shower, but before she would eat she rang the hospital, listening with strained concentration as the Sister in Charge told her that Nick's conditon had not changed and that she was not to come back until the next morning. Yes, the calm voice reassured her, if there was any change at all she would be rung.

Her eyes filled with tears. She put the receiver down and whispered, 'Oh God! He's so little——'

'He is a valiant fighter,' Alex said curtly. 'Come, eat. You need to keep your strength up.'

Amber forced herself to eat, prosciutto with the apricot contrast of fresh papaya flown in that day from the tropics, and superb fish, terakihi en papillote; she even drank a little wine, a Chardonnay with a subtle flavour from the South Island, but refused coffee. Alex was withdrawn, the massive reserve he could affect preventing her from seeing beyond anything but the courteous surface. Incurious, still sluggish with exhaustion, she followed his lead and spoke of nothings, until he said abruptly, 'Go back to bed, Amber.'

She did as she was told, and slept like the dead for a few hours until she was woken by the harsh, terrifying ring of the telephone from somewhere else in the suite.

Her heart gave a great leap in her breast; she lay frozen, as though by keeping absolutely motionless she could hold at bay the anguish that threatened. The soft 'ting' as the receiver was replaced drove the blood from

her cheeks; she wanted nothing more than to cower away
from the world like a dying animal, but Alex's voice at
the door of her room brought her head up from the
pillow. He said her name, softly so that if she was asleep
he wouldn't wake her.

In a strangled voice she whispered, 'Yes?'

He came noiselessly across the room to stand by the
bed. 'That was the hospital. The child has woken.'

Amber gave a great gasp, and fell into an agony of
tears, for the first few minutes uncaring that he held her
gently and stroked her bare back and her hair,
murmuring little soft words in Greek and French and
English to soothe her, until she had wept away the dread
and pain and terror. Then he gave her a handkerchief
and while she blew her nose he went to get her a face
cloth and a towel, waiting patiently while she mopped
up.

'Thank you,' she said inadequately, refusing to look at
him. 'I have to get up—I have to go to him. I should have
been there.'

He came with her, even came into the ward as she
asked eagerly what Nick had said.

'Not a lot,' the Sister in Charge said, smiling. 'He
demanded to see you, said he was hungry, and that he
had a headache. Then he went back to sleep.'

'Are you sure it's sleep?'

Amber couldn't help thinking that if she had asked the
question she would have received a somewhat crisp
answer, but all Alex got was an amused and very
confident smile.

'It's definitely sleep this time,' the Sister said. 'You'll
see the difference.'

Sure enough, it was obvious. It was not just that Nick
had colour in his skin, or that he had curled over on to his
side in his usual position, but one glance at the boyish
face and Amber could see that he had come back to her
from whatever lonely regions he had been wandering in.

'Well, he never really went away,' the Sister said cheerfully. 'Your talking helped, Mrs Stephanides. Even in a coma people respond to stimulus.'

Amber sat beside the bed and took the little paw in hers, blinking hard to keep the slow tears at bay until Alex said grimly, 'Come away, Amber. You've seen him, you know he's past the crisis. You need at least a night's sleep to function properly.'

'No,' she protested. 'I want to stay. He might wake up and want me.'

There was a silence and she looked up, to see her husband and the Sister looking at each other with the wary complicity of unlikely allies.

'He'll probably sleep until morning. You're still very tired,' the Sister began, only to be interrupted by Alex.

He spoke in the crisp, authoritative tones of the head of the Stephanides Corporation. 'Walk out, or I shall carry you,' he said. 'That is all the choice you have.'

Amber lifted Nick's hand to her trembling mouth and kissed it, then stood up. 'Tyrant,' she said weakly.

His black head inclined. 'We Greeks invented the word. Come, you will be rung as soon as he wakes up properly, or if his condition changes.'

Again he and the other woman exchanged glances. Amber's legs trembled, and instantly Alex flung an arm about her waist and ushered her through the door. She was conscious of the Sister's thoughtful expression, and then nothing more but extreme exhaustion, like a wave of darkness over both mind and body.

Before it carried her away she began, 'Matt . . .'

Tonelessly Alex replied, 'I shall see that he is told,'

When she awoke again it was late evening, a splendid rose and gold subtropical dusk, and she was lazily, deliciously languid, the blood pumping through her body in splendid vigour. She yawned and stretched, then said aloud, 'I'm hungry!'

Once more Alex appeared at the door. 'Are you,

indeed? I shall order dinner.'

Amber said shyly, 'Thank you.'

He gave her a long impenetrable look before he went back into the sitting-room and she lay back, tense in the great bed, listening to his deep autocratic voice as he spoke on the telephone. Once she breathed, 'Oh, thank God!' And knew that she was happy, but it came too soon after the rack of fear and tension to actually feel anything other than a vast relief.

When he came back into the room she said abruptly, 'I can't tell you how grateful I am to you.'

'Then do not try.' The words were steely and curt.

Amber watched from beneath her lashes as he came across to the bed, her heart thumping in her breast. Intense joy and the fierce pull of his magnetism combined forces to liberate her from the normal restraints of reason and logic.

He put a glass of chilled wine in her hand and commanded, 'Drink that.'

'Aren't you going to have some?'

'I think not.'

She bit her lip at the rejection, but the reckless delight that fizzed through her bloodstream persuaded her on. 'You must drink a toast because Nick has come back,' she persisted lightly. 'As a—a celebration of life.'

Alex looked down through his lashes at her. After long quivering moments the beautifully moulded mouth quirked into a smile, at once intimate and understanding, and strangely, not at all cynical. Very deeply he said, 'In that case, how can I refuse? We Greeks are firm believers in offerings to the gods, even the old ones who are officially dead. But I can think of another way to celebrate life, Amber.'

The wine was sweet and cool on her lips, like nectar down the dry harshness of her throat. She said nothing, but her mouth curved enigmatically and she drank deeply of the fragrant liquid.

'You must ask me,' whispered Alex, taking the glass from her to set his lips to the place where her mouth had touched. Above the rim his eyes gleamed, promising her pleasures that were dangerous, and irresistible.

Astonishing herself, Amber taunted softly, 'Why should I ask you? Why should I not just take?'

He drained the wine and laughed, half-mockingly, only to fall silent as she pushed free of the sheet and sat back on her haunches in front of him. Then lean brown fingers trembled slightly as he set the glass down and watched from narrowed eyes when she leaned forward and began unbuttoning his shirt.

She had forgotten how arousing it was to undress him, her small strong hands working swiftly at the buttons, then sliding beneath to the wide rough expanse of his chest. She re-learned the warm bulges of his muscles, pulled gently on the short tangle of hair, and with laughter and excitement glimmering in her eyes, leaned forward to suckle gently on the tight hard nub of his nipple.

His harshly indrawn breath was music; she rested her cheek against the swift rise and fall of his chest, and said, 'You always smell so good. Like warm male, half salt and half musk.'

'And you smell like a flower.' His voice was uneven, slow and absorbed as he lifted her chin and touched her throat with his mouth. 'Your own special flower, and yet you are definitely animal, warm and gold and erotic, like a golden cat, sinuous and sleek against me and beneath me and around me . . .'

She gasped, for he lowered his head to the pert tilt of her breasts and one hand held them together as he kissed the valley between and the pale slopes, bit with subtle delicacy at the tight aureoles while his hand slid across the sharp feminine angle of her hip and down to the curve of her buttock.

A strange sound rose in her throat, an almost exact

simulation of the purr of a cat, and she had to rest her
hands on his shoulders to keep herself upright because
her bones melted into honey, sweet and fiery and strong,
and she wanted more than anything else to feel the hard
possession of his body, the driving, primitive force that
was all masculine enfolded, engulfed, by her feminine
strength.

Alex looked up and smiled, a slow, provoking smile
that brought more colour to her throat and cheeks. Then
he ordered, 'Finish what you started. Undress me.'

Amber knelt up and pulled his shirt free. No shame, no
hesitation, slowed her hands. Nick hovered still in her
mind, she felt a mystical link between them, and some
ancient atavistic part of her brain persuaded her that by
making love, by summoning the energy of that most
basic, most imperative instinct, she and Alex would be
sending a surge of life-renewing power towards their son.

So she did not hurry. Indeed, it was impossible for her
to do so. This man who was her husband and the father of
her child was so beautiful, so potent in his masculinity,
that she could not have hurried if she tried. She kissed
him, touching his chest and the hard plane of his stomach
with fervent passion while her hands removed his
clothes, the silk shirt and the leather belt, then the
trousers, smoothing them down over narrow hips so that
she could see the heavy muscles of his thigh and rest her
head against the wall of his ribs while her hands tugged at
the sleek black briefs he wore.

And then she looked at him with shy delight, almost in
awe, and told him with husky sincerity, 'You're the most
beautiful man I know.'

He laughed at that, a little, and said slyly, 'But you
have not known many, my dove. I am not so flattered as I
could be if you were a woman of vast experience.'

She looked up into his face, but there was none of the
contempt she had grown accustomed to. Alex was
looking at her as though she was all that he had ever

wanted, and she pushed to the back of her mind the many
beautiful women he had been linked with. This seemed
right, as it had never done before. He would never know
that he was Nick's father, but she was glad that just this
once, the sexual attraction which blazed so strongly
between them should lead them towards such a trium-
phant affirmation of life.

She kissed the spot where the muscled plane of his
stomach met the curve of his hip, then slid back on to the
bed, glorying in the leaping glitter that fired his eyes as he
followed her down.

'Why?' he asked.

Amber shook her head, but when he repeated the
question she touched the sculptured line of his mouth
with an admonitory finger and said softly, 'Because—oh,
because it seems the right thing to do. Because Nick is
going to live.' She repeated what she had just thought. 'As
an affirmation of life.' Her laugh was a smoky little sound
in the dim room. 'Because I want you.'

His skin was hot and dry, almost feverish, like the
gleam of satisfaction in the half-closed eyes. 'So I have
the surrender I want?' he asked.

At that moment she could deny him nothing. 'Yes.'

He lay very still, his hands clasped around the pale
fragility of her shoulders. She could read nothing from
his expression: he seemed to have gone a long way away
from her into himself. Then the severe line of his mouth
relaxed; he said something in Greek and bent his head so
that his mouth lay against her breast.

'A sacrifice to the gods, I think. A thanksgiving . . . So
be it. Show me how much you want me,' he commanded
imperatively.

She had forgotten. Or perhaps maturity brought with it
a richer appreciation of the senses. Whatever it was, she
discovered anew the marvellous symmetry of a man's
body, the potent sorcery of skin over muscle, of long
powerful limbs, the sensual magic of male scent and the

force of masculine aggression, muted by regard for her
feminine frailty yet barely controlled. As her hands
rediscovered the shape and textures of his body she
gloried in the knowledge that he ached for her as she did
for him, that her soft little gasps were echoed in the deep
rasping breaths he took.

At last he groaned, 'Enough!' and lifted his head to
capture a sensitive nipple, drawing it into the voracious
depths of his mouth. Amber's bright head fell back on to
the pillow; she gave a long primitive moan as his skilful
fingers formed the soft contours of her breast, bronze
against palest gold and cream, masculine darkness
against the pallor of her woman's skin, which flushed
suddenly with colour as she trembled in ecstatic
recognition.

Oh, she thought desperately, she had forgotten so
much! Heat built in her veins, in the zones of greatest
sensitivity, beneath her skin and at the fork of her body,
a rushing tide of flame and need. She could hear herself
whispering his name with the simple-minded intensity of
a priestess of some old wicked religion, and she
shuddered as his tormenting mouth moved like a wildfire
across the smooth curves and tight planes of her body.

'Ah, Alex,' she breathed, stroking his shoulders and
the place at the back of his head where his crisp curls met
his nape. 'I want you so much . . .'

He rested his face on her stomach, sliding his hands
beneath her. 'You taste of flowers,' he said thickly.
'Sweet as springtime, more intoxicating than wine. I
have remembered it all these years.'

Some note of pain in his voice tore into her. She
whispered, 'Oh yes, I know, Alex. Forget everything but
this . . .'

She was wild for him, her body clenched in an agony of
the strangest desire, painful with the need to give
everything of herself to the ravishing force of their
passion. A gasp escaped her as he moved with the steely

grace she had not forgotten and thrust, deep, deep, making himself master of the flame and need that was her body. She gave herself up to the sensations which held her in thrall, and rocketed with him into a region where all else was forgotten but the necessity to give until she was drained, and take all that he imposed on her, the soaring, galloping ecstasy, and the final release, shattering, almost impersonal in its rhythm and power.

Afterwards, lying exhausted beneath him, she said in a slurred voice, 'Thank you.'

He moved away, turning on his side so that he could see her face. Her eyes were glazed and empty, and she was breathing in the deep pants of one who has endured extreme challenge. With a shaking hand he traced the edge of her mouth and the wet expanse of her forehead, the small whorls of her ears, and then the long, graceful line of her throat. His face was dark and withdrawn, his heavy lids hiding the thoughts behind them, and there were dark circles under his eyes.

'Go to sleep,' he said quietly.

Amber never found out what had happened to the meal he had ordered, for when she woke again it was morning, and he was shaving in the bathroom. For a few dreamy minutes she lay listening to the sound of his razor with a smile of feline satisfaction on her mouth. She should have been appalled at what she had done, but she was not; in the context of the night and its events their lovemaking had been natural and necessary. And she shivered as she thought of it, of the supreme delight he had given her so that she felt the most delicious repletion.

But, 'Enjoy it,' she told herself, 'because it's the last time you'll feel this way.'

The telephone at the side of the bed beckoned; she rang through to the hospital and had the incomparable delight of hearing the Sister on duty say that Nick had slept peacefully all night and was now waiting impatiently for her to come.

'I'll be along as soon as I've had breakfast,' she said, her voice velvet with happiness.

The soft buzz of the electric razor stopped; Alex appeared in the doorway, naked except for a towelling robe, his lean form glowing with energy and force, and Amber couldn't hide her joy when she told him what she had learned.

He nodded, his eyes as piercing as shards of crystal. 'I have talked to the doctor. He tells me that it will be at least a month before the child recovers.'

She sat very still, looking at him with suspicion.

'Until then I shall stay with you.' He came over and sat on the side of the bed, an inexorable hand moving the sheet down so that he could see the smooth curves of her breasts. 'As your husband,' he added smoothly, and stopped her instinctive protest by holding the sheet in place around her hips.

Amber knew that the colour fled from her skin. 'No!' she said harshly, then bit her lip at the unkind mockery that gleamed in his smile.

'Oh yes, Amber *mou*,' he returned, and bent his head and kissed her, leisurely exploring the soft pulsing hollow at the base of her throat. With his lips barely touching her skin he murmured, 'Last night you invited me into your bed, as I always knew you would. Now I will learn to sate myself in you, and then I will leave you and never see you, never touch you again. No, do not waste time in protest. I have made up my mind, and there is nothing you can do to change it.'

He was right. Amber's eyes closed in despair as she realised that the night before she had succumbed to the oldest lure of all, relief after intolerable strain. That was why war and sex went together, so that in the softness and oblivion of women men could forget the beastliness of what they had been forced to endure and do. Last night she too had wanted oblivion, craved it like a drug, and she had sought it the only way she knew how. And she had delivered herself into his hands.

Tonelessly she said, 'I can only assume that raping me will give you some sort of perverted satisfaction.'

Alex laughed, and his mouth swooped, touched the very edge of her nipple. Sharp spears of sensation pierced her body. Her breath hurt in her lungs; she could not prevent the telltale hardening of the nub, and he said with a menacing charm, 'I do not have to rape you, my dearest. I think that in spite of his very masculine attractions your cousin is not a good lover. Last night you seduced me, you were greedy for love, you gave yourself up to it with a ferocity which was almost frightening. A woman who enjoys her lover does not behave like that.'

Pain and pleasure were inextricably mixed. Amber opened her eyes and looked down at the crisp dark curls and the stark, chiselled profile at her breast. She shuddered, because in that instant she realised that she loved him. After all these years, after living with him and hating him and bearing his child, after disillusion and pain, she had learned to love this man.

A painful smile turned into a grimace. She said quietly, 'Last night I was not myself, as you're very well aware. I was crazy with relief.'

'Perhaps, but you knew what you were doing.' Alex's hand cupped the soft rise of her breast, gentle yet merciless. 'You used your emotions as a cover for the fact that you want me. I find your shame a little amusing. I am not ashamed to admit that I want you, that I only have to look at you and my loins ache, I want to take you, to make love to you in every way there is.'

Amber's voice shook as she replied, 'Then why do you want to sate yourself in me until you no longer want me?'

She felt his smile. 'You know why, Amber.'

'Yes, I do. To punish me. And because that's all you believe women are good for.'

'Ah no, I believe that women make very good mothers.' His voice altered in a way she couldn't discern

and he touched her stomach and the bowl of her hips
with a considering hand. 'You are an excellent mother, I
do not even try to deny that. Strong and patient and
brave. Would you love a child of mine as much as you
love Nick?'

Her heart stopped in her breast. Conception was
possible—not probable, because her cycle was a little
advanced, but it could happen. And if it did . . . She
swallowed, and heard the sound harshly reverberating in
her throat. It seemed an age until she could say levelly, 'I
don't think I could dislike a child.'

'I thought so.' Alex lifted his head swiftly, so swiftly
that she thought he must see and understand the alarm in
her expression, but there was nothing but an indolent
satisfaction in his face as he leaned back against the
pillows and yawned. 'I am tired,' he remarked, and before
Amber could answer, he idly pulled at one of the curls
against her ear and said, 'As for the other, I would like
very much to believe that women are capable of love and
self-sacrifice on behalf of their men, but I have not come
across very many who showed signs of such altruism.'

'You meet the wrong women.'

'Perhaps.' He shrugged. 'I learned early that women
save their deepest emotions for their children. And that
most women are prepared to sell anything, if the price is
high enough.'

She said warily, 'I realise you've probably seen more
greed than most men, but you've exploited women
unmercifully, you and your sex, for thousands of years.
Can you blame us for using the only weapons we possess
in our efforts to even things up?'

'I do not blame you for anything as I have had much
pleasure from your choice of weapons. But I do not
expect any more than you are prepared to give. I am a
realist.'

'You're a hopeless cynic,' she said sadly. 'I feel sorry
for you. I don't judge all men by you and my father.'

'You have found a superman in your cousin?' Each word was an acid little taunt.

Amber was sorely tempted, but the power he wielded so ruthlessly kept her restrained. 'Matt is a dear,' she said wryly, 'but he can be just as macho and ruthless as you are.'

Alex's fingers on the curl tightened. He slid his hand into her hair and used it to tilt her face back so that he could see into it. She looked at him fearlessly, seeing the sculptured planes and angles of his face oddly foreshortened. A drenching, overwhelming sweetness held her in thrall; she wondered how it would be to have him look at her with the eyes of love, even as she knew that it would never happen. He was too cynical, too accustomed to taking his pleasure from the women who fluttered around him.

'I do not wish to see you with your cousin until I am tired of you,' he said without emotion, his eyelids lowered to hide his thoughts.

'What do you mean?'

He smiled and shrugged, lazily complacent. 'I do not share, my dear. Anything.'

Colour flooded her cheeks. She gave a twist and freed herself from him, getting up from the bed with unconscious dignity. 'You needn't worry,' she said shortly as she grabbed her robe and belted it around her. 'Anyway, he's still in hospital, for heaven's sake!'

Alex waited until she had almost got to the door of the bathroom before he said silkily, 'A broken leg would not stop me from taking you. If I see you look at him with eyes of desire, Amber, I shall consider our bargain negated.'

She swallowed sickly but managed to say, 'I give you my word that that won't happen.'

'Perhaps,' he said, gently musing, 'I was wrong when I said I had never seen a woman make a sacrifice for her man. You are prepared to act the whore for your cousin.

But it is hardly a difficult choice, is it? Clearly he does not satisfy you, and you cannot deny that I do.'

Amber left the room to the sound of his soft laughter.

She tried again in the car on the way to the hospital. 'Won't the Corporation go bankrupt if you aren't there to control things? When we were married you spent most of the time running around the world taking care of it.' In spite of her control she couldn't prevent the sour note in her voice.

Alex chose to ignore it, lifting broad shoulders in an elegant shrug. 'That was because my father had over-extended the business. Now I have managers I can trust, or who fear me too much to cheat, and I can delegate much of the work. And modern electronics make keeping contact an easy task. So I can stay here for as long as I wish.'

His smile was edged and mocking, taunting her with her impotence.

Amber swallowed, remembering last night and its shattering result, her realisation that she loved him. The weeks ahead were going to be painfully sweet, a kind of honeyed poison which would infect her for the rest of her life.

She dragged her eyes free of his and had to listen to his soft, pleased chuckle with no visible signs of pain.

Again he came with her when she went into the ward, his crystalline eyes aloof as he looked at the child he would never know was his. Nick was lying with his head turned to the door, but he appeared to be dozing. He didn't react until Amber took his hand. Then as though her touch was a signal he opened his eyes, large and a clear, dark grey, and looked at her.

'Hi,' she whispered, trying to smile and keep back tears.

'Mum?' He frowned, then relaxed. 'Mum, how's Uncle Matt? The nurse said he hurt his leg.'

'He broke it, but he's fine. Do you remember what happened?'

He shook his head. His hand tightened on hers as he whispered, 'I remember swimming in the morning, and then we went for a walk. What did happen?'

While she told him he listened with his eyes fixed on her, frowning slightly before he asked, 'How did we get here?'

'In a helicopter, love. The police flew you in.'

Nick sighed gustily, the very picture of disappointment. 'I wish I could remember. Trust me to be out to it when we come in a police helicopter!'

The doctor arrived, all smiles, and said in a jolly voice, 'Yes, you look a lot more like yourself than you did this time yesterday, Nick. Now we'll send your parents outside so we can do a few tests on you, young man.'

Outside Amber found that she was shaking, the tears coursing down her cheeks in a silent agony of emotion. Alex put her into a chair and waited while she mopped up, responding to her stifled apology with a curt nod. He was frowning yet abstracted, and when she had recovered her control he said brusquely, 'I have things to do. Will you be all right if I leave you here?'

Sudden radiance lit her face. 'Oh, nothing can go wrong now!'

His eyes drooped. 'So the sacrifice will be worth it?'

She said defensively, dry-mouthed, 'Any woman would sacrifice almost anything for the life of her child, you know.'

'And if the sacrifice is enjoyable, so much the easier,' said Alex sardonically as he swung on his heel and left her.

Amber watched the ripple of interest among the hospital personnel with resignation and a bitter amusement. Once she had felt a certain smugness at the avid interest that always followed Alex's progress; now she hated it.

Once he had gone and the ward had simmered down she got to her feet, squaring her chin at the man who had just left. It was going to be half an hour before she could go back in to Nick, so she went cautiously down to see Matt. After that final threat from Alex she did not want to be caught visiting her cousin, but she needed to tell him herself how Nick was.

He was lying in bed looking grim, and when he turned his head at her arrival his eyes were bleak. She bent to drop a kiss on his cheek and sat down, suddenly conscious of the soft fullness of her lips, the telltale glow that Matt would recognise. Hastily, feeling oddly like a traitor, she told him how Nick was.

His glance was perceptive and a little ironic. 'I knew, of course, that he'd come out of the coma—the Sister came through with the news yesterday. Apparently Stephanides gave instructions that I was to be told.' His smile was a mere movement of his lips, wry and almost entirely lacking in humour. 'The least he could do, seeing that I'm supposed to be Nick's father!'

'I'm sorry,' whispered Amber.

She avoided his eyes and found herself pleating the skirt of the shirtwaister Matt's housekeeper had packed and forwarded to Auckland. 'I've made such a mess of everything, Matt, but I didn't know what else to do! Alex doesn't love me, but he doesn't like to think that—well, that——'

'That we're lovers. No. Looking from his point of view it's put him in an almost impossible situation. He seems to be a damned possessive man, yet he's forced to behave with some degree of complaisance to the man he believes to be his wife's lover, as well as the child of that liaison. Most men would find the situation intolerable.'

'Possessiveness was all he ever felt.' Amber's voice was remarkably steady. 'But I have to agree that he's behaved with grace and dignity in an awkward situation. It's just as well that he never fancied that he was in love with me.'

Some hint of the desolation in her heart must have shown, because Matt reached out to touch her cheek. 'Cheer up,' he said in his gentlest voice. 'It's not the end of the world.'

'Everything's so complicated,' she said, shivering.

He watched her keenly as he suggested, 'You could tell him the truth.'

'Oh no!' She shuddered, her face blanched, and went on urgently, 'I wondered—when Nick looked so ill I wondered if I should, it seemed so unfair to Alex not to know, but—I still think I did the right thing. When he goes back home he's determined to divorce me and then he can marry and have more children. Whom he will bring up to be tyrants, if they're sons, and docile if they're daughters.'

Each word cut to the heart. She evaded Matt's penetrating scrutiny and deliberately stilled her fingers, knowing even as she did so that she had betrayed herself. It was impossible to live, however platonically, with a man for nine years and not have him understand you.

After a long moment Matt said quietly, 'I see. And you, Amber? What will you do then?'

Her look was startled. She said, 'I don't know,' in an oddly breathless voice.

'You could,' said Matt calmly, 'marry me.'

She was not as surprised as she might have been, but her eyes filled with tears and she said in muffled tones, 'No, you deserve someone who'll love you with all her heart. I love you, but not the way you should be loved.'

He said quietly after a short pause, 'Well, we can give it time. In the meantime, rest assured that I'll back you up.'

'Even though you hate it.'

He leaned back against his pillows, lean and somehow remote, his eyes lashed against her glance. 'I can't help thinking how I would feel in a similar situation,' he told her drily. 'Whatever I think of Stephanides' morals, I have to admire the man. He could have left you to cope with this alone, but he stayed and has given you what support he can. However, it's not my business. Now tell me all about Nick.'

Amber told him, her face alight, and he listened and watched her, wondering if she had any idea how attractive she was. It was not so much that she was beautiful, although he thought so, but that her face was so expressive, her smile warm and free from guile, honest and candid.

When she had finished he asked on an impulse, 'Amber, why are you so determined to keep the truth from him? What did he do that's made you so determined to keep Nick free of his influence?'

She flinched and the lovely radiance died out of her face. 'I don't—no,' she said with sudden determination, 'you should know, it's the least I can do, seeing that I've embroiled you in the whole affair. I think I've told you before that my father had no time for me. He was far too busy being a tycoon to waste time on his wife and child. When I was introduced to Alex it was like—oh, it was just as if he lit fires in my blood! I fell all the way. He was so handsome I almost fainted when he kissed me, and he wooed me as if I were the most exquisite creature he'd ever seen. I thought we were fated for each other.'

Her smile twisted into self-derision. 'Talk about green! So we were married, and we had a fabulous honeymoon in the Bahamas and I thought I was going to live happily ever after with this wonderful Adonis who adored me as much as I loved him. Then we went back to Crete and I discovered that I was expected to share the enormous house with his father and stepmother. Alex travelled a lot, and Irene, his stepmother, had absolutely no intention of stepping down from her position as châtelaine.'

'Why didn't you travel with Stephanides?'

'I did, a couple of times, but it was hopeless. I was just

a nuisance. Alex worked all hours of the day and night, the last thing he wanted was a lonely, bored little wife trailing around after him. His friends, his business acquaintances, were sophisticated people. I was still a schoolgirl. I was shy and awkward and overwhelmed. So after the first couple of trips I stayed behind.'

'And?'

She smiled ironically. 'Irene found me boring and a nuisance too.' She stopped, remembering. 'I couldn't speak Greek, so Alex's father forbade anyone to speak English to me, or answer me if I spoke to them in English. I can recommend it as a way to learn a language quickly!'

Matt's voice was low and deadly. 'And your husband allowed him to isolate you like that?'

Strangely Amber felt impelled to explain. 'Alex loved his father, and respected him enormously. A Greek man is head of his household, and Alex's father was one of the old school. He thought women were useful in the house, and that that was where they should be. I honestly don't think he believed women could be as intelligent as men. He wasn't unkind, he just didn't understand. Alex used to speak French with me when we were alone.'

When they made love. Always when they made love, even on their honeymoon. And last night too; she had to push away the memory of his impeded voice groaning out his hunger, his need, the heated impress of his body, and the soaring rapture that submerged her at his possession.

'Probably because he had a French mistress,' she said steadily. 'Her name was Gabrielle, and he'd installed her in a discreet villa not far away about a year before we were married. His stepmother told me all about her; she pointed her out to me in Iraklion one day. She was tall and voluptuous, and she had a face like Aphrodite and hair like moonbeams. She was the most beautiful woman I've ever seen. Her walk was a miracle; I swear every man in the street watched as she walked past. Believe me, I was no competition.'

All her dead dreams were in her face. Matt said nothing, but his eyes were savage as he watched her.

After a moment Amber gave a set little smile. 'Funny, it still hurts. Anyway, I was too stupid, too naïve to behave with any decorum. Or any manifestations of common sense, come to that. I confronted him, filled with righteous indignation.'

'And what did he do?'

'Admitted it.' She was wry and amused and sad all at once. 'So he got the full works—tears, wailings of betrayal, pleas to go home—oh, you can't believe how badly I behaved! To no avail. Alex was cool and polite and implacable. So I demanded that he choose between us. He gave me a wolfish grin and told me that I was his wife and that was an end to it.'

Matt said something short and succinct and unrepeatable.

Amber lifted an eyebrow, suddenly tired. 'Oh, from his point of view he had every right to expect me to put up with it. The situation was by no means unusual. In fact, in the circles he moved in, that was the norm. My father, too ... And that's why I don't want Nick to grow up there. I can't tell you how betrayed I felt, what kind of hell of disillusion I went through——'

'You don't need to,' he said gently. 'You arrived out here a month or so later. I remember how long it took you to laugh again.'

'If I thought that Nick might grow up feeling he had the right to behave the same way I—well, I think I'd be sorry I'd had him. He's much better off here, with some hope of a normal way of life, a normal outlook.'

Matt nodded, but she could tell that she hadn't managed to convince him. How men stick together, she thought, conscious of a bone-deep weariness licking through her body. And how stupid I am, seducing Alex, laying myself open to yet more pain and anguish. But at least, she reminded herself slyly, it was she who had done the seducing, not Alex. She had managed to retain a little pride.

Matt broke into her thoughts by asking, 'So what happens now?'

She couldn't tell him about the bargain she had struck. He would be furious that she had tried to shelter him, wounded in that most vulnerable part of a man's character, his pride. But he must have seen something, because he suddenly caught her wrist, long fingers biting into the fragile bones.

'Amber! What——'

She touched her tongue to her lip and said desperately, 'Matt, there's nothing that can be done. It's——'

Smooth as cream, Alex said from the doorway, 'Can you not understand that Amber belongs to me?' He strolled into the room, challenge glittering in his eyes, etched in his face as he faced the man he considered to be his adversary. 'Amber is mine,' he said softly, dangerously. 'She always has been.'

CHAPTER EIGHT

APPALLED, Amber held her breath. What was Matt, every bit as proud, going to reply to the gauntlet Alex had just flung at him?

She should have known better than to panic. Matt turned a thoughtful look on her, read the appeal in her eyes, and although Alex's arrogance clearly grated on him said mildly enough, 'That decision is Amber's. And I'm not going to start a brawl here. We can discuss this later.'

Alex said from between his teeth, 'Perhaps you did not understand what I said. Amber is my wife. I am sleeping with her. I have every intention of making love to her until I go. Then, perhaps, you can have her back—if you still want her.'

Matt looked at him with icy scorn. 'You're a swine, Stephanides. You couldn't leave her to be happy, could you, you had to pamper that inflated ego of yours by seducing her so that she could be miserable again!'

His abuse was met by an insolent, feral grin. Alex said gently, 'But I did not seduce her, that was never my intention. She seduced me.' He spread his hands, shrugging in a parody of worldliness, and his cold eyes never left Matt's face. 'I am a normal man. When I am offered a pretty woman I usually take her.'

Matt had regained control. His leonine features were a cold mask; he looked for long seconds at Alex before letting his glance drift to Amber's horrified face. And he smiled sympathetically and said to her, 'Well, you did tell me what he was like. I must confess I thought you exaggerated, but clearly I was wrong.'

Alex didn't bother to hide his contempt. He stared at Matt, obviously dumbfounded at his calmness, then turned on his heel and left them.

Matt said evenly, 'No marks for guessing his thoughts! That I have to be the weakest man he's ever come in contact with!'

In a panic, because if she told him the truth Matt would insist on protecting her and put himself in jeopardy, Amber took refuge in a cliché. 'The Greeks are also possessive—even with goods they consider damaged.'

She looked into her cousin's austere countenance with all the limpid conviction she could summon, and saw his suspicion fade a little.

'I hope you know what you're doing,' he said at last, brows still knitted as he watched her. 'I know that you've always kept a candle lit for him,' he went on, smiling narrowly at her astonishment. 'My dear, no one, man or woman, stays faithful to a memory for nine years unless some extraordinarily powerful emotion existed in the first place. I don't blame you, even I can see what the man's got. But are you sure this is what you want? From what you've said you know damned well he's not the sort it's safe to love.'

Amber gave a twisted smile, grateful that he hadn't pointed out to her what a fool she was to get involved with Alex again. 'I think I should get him out of my system. Then I might be able to live a more normal life.'

Apparently she was convincing enough, for he relaxed and returned her smile with wry affection and understanding. 'I know the feeling. With him you had fireworks; it's difficult to settle for anything less dangerous.' He frowned, watching her from beneath his lashes. 'You've grown up a lot, matured into a strong woman, but I remember how shattered you were when you arrived. I wouldn't like that to happen again.'

She said earnestly, trying to reassure herself as well as him, 'Nothing's changed, Matt. I won't be living with him again, so the fact that he's constitutionally unable to be faithful isn't going to worry me. I'm almost ten years older now, and a lot wiser. But I'm incredibly sorry I got you into this.'

Matt grinned with reckless, flashing charm. 'Hell, love, think nothing of it. I don't mind that he considers me so besotted with you I don't care who else you sleep with! It's all for a good cause.'

Matt really didn't mind. Like Alex he possessed the kind of bone-deep confidence which gave him complete self-assurance. He didn't have to prove himself to anyone. They were two of a kind, strong and disciplined with a concentrated authority which made them formidable.

And that, of course, was why Matt must never know about the threats Alex had used to force her into this charade.

Amber looked at him with her love and gratitude clearly written in her expression, and at that moment Alex arrived back, face as black as a thunderstorm. It didn't seem possible, but it deepened as he took in Amber's sudden involuntary step away from her cousin; nor was it lessened by the small ironic twist to Matt's mouth.

Very softly, Alex said one word—just her name, and she found herself going across to him. For a long moment he held Matt's eyes, his cold and steel-coloured, daring him to object. A strange expression flitted across Matt's aquiline features, but he exercised his considerable control and said nothing.

It was like the stand-off in a Western, Amber found herself thinking, but this was no make-believe. Menace crackled across the still air, and met a solid, calm resistance from Matt, force against immovable strength.

Neither man backed down. And in those long tense moments, Amber saw the birth of a reluctant respect. Strangely, she was the one who defused the situation. She said quietly, 'I'll have to go back to Nick. As soon as I can I'll consult the doctors here to see when they think he'll be fit enough to move. We'll need to be able to get back quickly to the hospital if anything—if he needs to at any time.'

It was strangely comforting to see the two bristling males ease their silent confrontation in the interests of a small boy.

'I came to tell you that he is back in the ward and asking for you,' Alex said remotely, taking her by the elbow.

Amber expected him to say something sneering about Matt's attitude, but he did not speak all the way back to the ward. When they arrived back he came in with her as Nick turned an impatient face her way.

Emotion threatened to choke her; she had to clear her throat before she could ask, 'How's your head?'

He grinned. 'Sore, but it's getting better. Mum, when can I go home?'

'Oh, love,' she said on a half laugh, 'I don't know yet, but not for a few days at least. That was some crack you had, you know.'

He wriggled, small-boyishly, and directed an interested look towards Alex, standing silent and formidable behind Amber. Nick's mouth quirked as he said in his politest manner, 'How do you do. I'm Nick Duncan.'

Alex bent and shook his hand. 'And I am Alex Stephanides.'

Nick's face lit up. 'I've heard of you,' he said eagerly. 'You used to race rally cars, didn't you? I read where someone said you could have been one of the best if you hadn't given it up. Why did you, Mr Stephanides?'

Alex smiled. 'Alas, it was interfering with my work. I

was becoming far too interested in rallying and not enough in making a living.'

Nick clearly thought he had made the wrong decision, but was too polite to say so. 'I'm going to race when I grow up,' he said. 'I can drive everything on the station except the bulldozer, but I'm not allowed out on the road with them until I'm old enough to get a licence.'

Every word from her son, every movement of his expressive face, seemed to Amber to point up the similarity between the two males. She had always thought Nick took after her side of the family, and indeed in colouring he did, with his warm tortoiseshell hair and skin which was the warm gold of his Northern ancestors, not the Mediterranean tan of his father, but she realised now that his features were almost as classical as Alex's; in time to come they would resemble each other very strongly.

Made very uneasy by this, she said as coolly as she could, 'Nick, Mr Stephanides is a busy man, he can't stay chatting with you, I'm afraid.'

Nick looked a little disappointed, but he accepted it with his normal sunny nature. Acutely conscious of the sharply penetrating glance Alex bestowed on her, Amber felt her heart miss a beat as he said, 'I am glad to have met you, Nikos. Perhaps I will see you again.'

When he was gone Nick said reproachfully. 'You shouldn't have chased him away, Mum, I'm not very sick at all really.'

Amber said something in reply and made him chuckle, but all through the day she spent at his side she felt her nerves begin to stretch. If Alex was going to make a habit of looking in on Nick, how long would it be before that altogether too percipient brain began to make connections and come up with the truth?

It took a little effort, but she managed to thrust her worries to the back of her mind. Still a little lightheaded with relief, she spent the rest of the day at Nick's bedside, keeping him happy and occupied, leaving only after he was asleep. To find that, splendidly ignoring the nurses who kept sending appreciative sideways glances his way, Alex was waiting for her.

Her eyes clashed with his, glittering and metallic, and an unknown fear spread cold wings over her. Suddenly feeling very alone, she went quietly with him through the hospital, so familiar now, smiling automatically at the staff they met, and allowed herself to be put into the car.

It was dark outside and had been raining, and over everything in the thick warm air there was the smell of the sea. In the foyer of the hotel a frangipani bush held clusters of creamy-pink scented flowers up to the velvet sky beside a pool which held a group of great koi carp, petulant and glowing as their tails flicked in their endless silent odyssey.

Amber was suddenly vividly aware of the man beside her; she saw that awareness in the eyes of those who watched them. Alex did not set out to attract attention or the desirous speculative glances of women, he did it just by being himself, authoritative and forceful, his striking good looks spreading a veneer of civilisation over the barbaric hunter he was at heart.

As they waited for the elevator to descend he said suddenly, 'I am not likely to corrupt the child, you know.'

She took in a sharp breath of pure panic, and stiffened as he registered the fact. 'I know.' Inspiration born of fear led her to say, 'I'm so afraid he'll get too tired and slip back into a coma.'

She looked up into his face and immediately wished she hadn't. He was watching her with the cold guarded look of a predator. 'Is that likely to happen?'

The elevator doors hushed closed behind them. 'No. I asked the specialist,' Amber admitted in a small voice, studying the floor. 'He said it was most unlikely. I felt a fool.'

'He is,' he said aloofly, 'a charming child. You must be proud of him.'

For some reason—guilt, almost certainly—Amber wanted to give him some insight into his son. She said, 'He can be a little demon when he wants to be, but mostly he's very easy to live with, although he's as stubborn as a pig when he gets an idea in his head. He's not above making use of that charm to get his own way.'

Her voice trailed into silence when Alex looked down at her with ice in his eyes. By then they had reached the penthouse and she was glad to get out of the confines of the lift and into the suite, where there was room to avoid him.

Dinner was eaten in the suite; a silent meal. Afterwards, while Alex spoke on the telephone in his bedroom, Amber read the newspaper, then went across to the window and looked out over the city and the harbour. A depression gripped her; she leaned her forehead against the glass and felt the tears aching in her eyes. She should be on top of the world, unable to contain her relief and happiness, yet all she could think of was the mess some people made of their lives. Reaction, of course, but recognising it didn't seem to help her snap out of it at all. She looked down the avenue of years ahead and found them bathed in grey.

Alex finished whatever was keeping him on the telephone, for he appeared behind her now and asked with impatience crackling through the words. 'What are you doing? Do you want to go down for a drink?'

It was important that he not see her tears. She managed to say in a fairly convincing voice, 'Yes, that would be pleasant. I'll get a——'

His hand on her shoulder urged her around. For a long

moment he searched her face, his own hardening. 'Why are you crying?'

She shook her head, afraid at the total lack of emotion in his face and voice. 'I'm not——'

'Don't lie. I can see the tears.'

Amber bit her lip and tried again, with the truth this time. 'Reaction. I'm coming down, and it's hard. I tell myself I should be over the moon, but all I feel is a grey exhaustion. Stupid, isn't it?'

'I think so. Perhaps something that is not so stupid is that you are missing your cousin.'

His tone warned her, but she said quietly, 'No.'

'Then you will not mind coming with me.'

Bewildered, she replied, 'I'd already agreed——'

He touched her cheek, and then ran a thumb across her bottom lip. He was smiling, but his eyes were flat and deadly. 'I have changed my mind. I don't want a drink. We'll go to bed instead.'

Amber was afraid. There was something ominous about his calmness, something that reminded her of the perilous pause in the heart of a hurricane. She opened her mouth to object, then caught the unspoken words back on an indrawn breath. He said nothing, just watched her with that flat stare, but she could see how useless any protest would be.

'Very well,' she said in a thin voice, refusing to give him the pleasure of having her object. She walked across the room and into her bedroom, took off her clothes and got into the bed, repressing with willpower and determination the shudders that attacked her. Her hands were clenched at her side; she shut her eyes and told herself steadily that she had made love with him only a few hours ago, that there was nothing to be afraid of. For some reason he was angry, and he probably wouldn't be gentle, but he was no monster of cruelty.

She heard him moving about and then her already

rigid body tensed further, almost to the point of pain, as he slid under the light covering beside her. She made no movement towards him, just lay there holding her breath.

'You look like little Red Riding Hood at the moment she realised that her granny had metamorphosed into a wolf,' drawled Alex. 'I do not intend to eat you, Amber.'

Her jaw relaxed a little, enough for her to say, 'I know that.' She didn't recognise her voice, and her throat was so tight that she had to swallow to clear it before the words came out.

'But you are right to be apprehensive,' he said silkily.

Amber's skin prickled, but when it came the touch of his hand was maddeningly soft, a drift of gentleness from her chin to the hollow in her throat. It was cowardly to lie there like a naughty child, so she opened her eyes. There was no expression in his face and his lashes were lowered, hiding whatever emotions lurked behind them. the chiselled features were even and calm, the beautifully moulded mouth relaxed and half-smiling.

Why, then, did she feel the menace radiating from him? Why was she so frightened that her mind couldn't formulate thoughts?

She whisperd his name, but he ignored her plea, if that was what it was, and that soft soothing stroke of his fingers went on rediscovering the smooth golden skin on her shoulders, the sweep of slender arm and the gentle rise of her breasts.

Her eyes lingered on his shoulders, wide enough to block the world out, then unfocused, but that was a mistake, because then all that she had to concentrate on was the slow, disturbing slide of his fingers over her skin in an erotic tactile enchantment of her senses. So she gave her head a little shake and fixed her eyes on his still, absorbed face.

He smelt faintly of salt, warm and intermingled with

the masculine aura of musk that dragged at her nostrils. The light from the lamp gilded his silhouette, picked up the dark scattering of hairs on his arms and the tight crisp curls on his well-shaped head. Amber felt a sudden hot deliquescence in the vulnerable area between her thighs. Her mouth trembled and then firmed as a long tremor swept over her sensitised skin.

'Look,' he murmured, 'my hand is dark against your skin. If I were a painter I would use a mirror to paint us like this, and I would call the picture 'Contrasts' and keep it for my eyes only, and burn it before I die.'

Amber's throat tightened so that she had to swallow before she could say huskily, 'I didn't know you went in for pornography.'

'Is that what you think it would be? I don't find anything pornographic in honest desire.'

Words hummed in her head, but she was unable to say them, her whole being dazed by the slow sensuous stroke of his fingers. She drew in a sharp breath as they curved around the soft swell of her breast; a pang of delicious anticipation shafted like lightning through her body. Her eyes were heavy and slumbrous; slowly she leaned her head sideways until her seeking mouth met the skin of Alex's shoulder.

She felt his shudder as though it was her own, and the reckless passion which only he evoked burst into life. Swiftly her hand ran from his shoulder to his waist, and across the hard angularity of his hip to the tight masculine buttocks. She pulled, and he laughed and without any further preliminaries moved over her, entering with one fierce thrust into the heated depths of her body.

Amber gasped, transfixed, and her lashes flew up to meet the searing need which blazoned forth on his face. She said his name, her hips rising, and then all conscious thought was suspended in an agony of sensation which took her to the edge of unconsciousness, suspended her for long ecstatic moments above the abyss, and then exploded into a satisfaction so intense that she found herself weeping in its slow aftermath.

'Hush,' he soothed when his breathing had slowed and he was able to lift his black head from her neck. 'Amber, don't cry.'

She gulped and said hesitantly, 'I'm sorry, I'm not—I'm perfectly all right. It's just that——' She broke off abruptly, but he was watching her and she saw the satisfaction open in his face.

'*He* is unable to give you that,' stated Alex flatly, defying her to deny it.

Amber said nothing, turning her head away, but his fingers turned cruel as they dragged her chin back. 'Look at me,' he insisted harshly. 'Look at me, Amber, and tell me that you respond like that in his bed.'

She bit her lips to still their quivering, paling at his low satisfied laughter.

'No, you cannot. He cannot give you pleasure so intense that you almost faint from it.'

'Sex isn't everything,' she protested weakly.

Alex smiled knowingly and bent his head to touch her lower lip with the very tip of his tongue. She should have been completely uninterested, but the tiny caress made her catch her breath, and she felt the heat of his breath as he laughed and whispered, 'Of course sex is not everything, but for a woman as highly sexed as you it is important. Is that why you seem to have nothing but a friendly affection for him? Can he not satisfy the fires in your blood, Amber *mou*? Never mind, I will show you what passion is like, and when you accept his lukewarm affection you will remember and perhaps you will fantasise and the fires might be a little quenched.'

Amber said bitterly, 'You're a swine.'

He grinned, lethal and vibrant with confidence in his

own sexuality. A dark brow lifted in a taunt as he answered, 'Because I make you forget him? Because you tremble when I touch you, and beg when I stop, and cry out when I take you? How is that my fault? Because you betray him every time you look at me? You are my wife, not his.'

He took her mouth in a hard, biting kiss, oppressing her with his knowledge of her reactions so that even as she flamed into action beneath him she understood the degradation he planned for her. Slowly, almost contemptuously, he kissed the throbbing hollow in her throat, the tender temples and at last the smooth heated silk of her breasts, laughing at her smothered moan and the jerky stiffening of her body.

Amber held out for only a few moments before the subtle drawing of his mouth on her breast made her relax into a sensual languor so intense that she squeaked when he slid on to his back and brought her to her side, half on the lean hardness of his body, half off.

'Now,' he commanded, 'make love to me.'

Later, when she was free of the spell he seemed to cast over her, she was ashamed at herself. Because in that moment, as she lay looking down into the cool smoky grey of his eyes, she vowed that just this once he was going to lose the massive restraint which kept him in control of even their most maddened moments. This time he was going to learn what a woman could do to his arrogant self-assurance.

Because she had little experience, she had to summon all her powers of invention, watch and listen and guess as she had never had to do in all her life before, and apply her own innermost desires and the insight of love to her seduction of him.

It was amazing, she found herself thinking, just how easily she could read him, and that her intense concentration on him and his reactions and needs wasn't stopping her body's reactions.

On the contrary, it was as though her sensual being fed on his response, flaming into life and action as she discovered a multitude of ways to drive him out of his mind, using her hands and the silken subtle flick of her mouth, the slow kiss of skin against skin. She thought then that it was ironic that she should learn her lesson so well when it was highly unlikely she would ever need this knowledge again.

At last he surrendered, groaning his submission at the same time as he pulled her on to him, his hands cruelly curving about her hips, his face flushed and contorted with desire and the depths of his eyes glazed with a passion he could not master in spite of his immense willpower.

Impaled by him, Amber gasped, her body transfixed and rigid as the unusual sensations overpowered thought. From beneath heavy lids his eyes were shining slivers of polished silver, opaque, merciless.

She shook her curls back and laughed, then began to move, using inbuilt knowledge from all the women in her ancestral tree, all of the wild free instincts, every understanding of that most basic urge, as she gave at once her strength and her weakness as a sacrifice to his sexuality. Only her love gave her the freedom to lose herself in his arms.

Quickly, so quickly she gasped again, the driving force of their union began to turn in on itself. Mesmerised, her eyes stayed fixed on the dark savagery of his face, but now her concentration was on the tides of sensation which were gathering in her, each surge more strong, more irresistible, until she could see nothing, feel nothing but the incredible need to flow with them, discover the unknown, the dangerous shore through the turbulence.

When at last it happened and the wave of rapture broke over her in a flood of fire and sensation she cried out, and was dimly aware of an answering cry from the man who held her upright.

Then she collapsed, boneless and exhausted, on to the heat and dampness of his body beneath her, and began to shake. Alex said nothing; he pulled her head into the sweat-streaked hollow of his neck and swallowed. Amber felt the muscles move as in a voice that was slow and thick he said, 'Go to sleep, Amber.'

Some time during the night he left, because when she woke in the morning all that remained of him was a note.

No salutation, no signature, just three sentences in his bold, curt writing. *I have to go. Please feel free to occupy this suite until your son is able to go home. You will be hearing from my lawyers soon.*

She should have expected it. She should have known. Alex was running true to form; loss of control equalled loss of face, and he struck back as he had nine years before when she had told him that she was not going to accept his conception of the role a wife should play in his life.

Only this time he had been a little more subtle.

Oh, he had warned her. In his own way he had played fair. She could not accuse him of anything but a lust for revenge which was stronger than the passion they made together. So she was going to have to endure the pain and bear the anguish without revealing any of it.

Strangely, it wasn't too difficult. She just packed her heart in ice, and if Matt watched her with concern she pretended not to see it, and Nick was too busy getting better to understand that his mother's heart was broken. But she knew now why she had fled so precipitately from her marriage, all those years ago. It was not the childish reaction to setbacks that Alex accused her of; it was because she had always known in some instinctive part of her that he had the power to hurt her so deeply she would never recover.

She had been too immature to understand then, but she had known that he was a man she could love; the loving had come late, she thought wearily, but it was like a hurricane in her heart, a fierce elemental passion which wrought a deep abiding change in her.

Then, one morning three months later when they were all back home, she woke and was sick, and she could no longer fool herself. She waited until the nausea faded, then went along to the breakfast-room, cold and shaking inside. Matt was gone, but Nick was still there, recounting to Mrs Crawford for the tenth time the details of his accident. Amber smiled at them both and slid into her chair, her eyes fixed on the teapot as if it was her one hope of salvation.

After a cup she felt much better, able to deal with Nick's high spirits, and his frequently repeated question, 'Mum, when can I play football again?'

'Today,' she said with composure.

He stared at her. 'Truly? Is that what the doctor said?'

'That, my darling, is what the doctor said.'

'Oh boy!' he breathed. 'I don't have to be careful any more?'

'No more so than usual.'

He whooped and slid down from the table, running into the kitchen to tell the housekeeper, and then out of the house to yell and laugh around the garden. Amber's smile faded; wretchedly she surveyed the tea in her cup and wondered what she was going to do now.

She dared not stay here. Apart from its being unfair to Matt, she was almost certain that Alex would be keeping her watched. Whether or not he had realised that she wasn't using any form of contraception, this time she would not be able to convince him that the child she carried was Matt's. Which left her with nothing to do but run.

Wearily she fought back tears. It was stupid to bawl;

she had known that pregnancy was possible ever since that first night. They were clearly very compatible, she and Alex. Aloud she said, 'It just doesn't seem fair.'

The following weeks were horrible. She was listless and enervated, finding it hard to do any of the work about the place, even the secretarial work which was so important to Matt.

He watched her, frowning, and once suggested that she might be suffering from delayed shock.

'Rubbish!' she retorted robustly.

'Then what's the matter with you? You've made three mistakes in this pedigree, and you had to rewrite a letter yesterday. It's not like you, Amber.' She looked away, and his voice hardened. 'Are you pining for Stephanides?'

She laughed at that, but without humour. Her first instinct had been to hide her condition from him, but she owed him too much to do that.

So she said bluntly, 'I'm pregnant.'

He said nothing, and she looked up into a face hard and angry. He said something she pretended not to have heard, then his expression softened and he looped a comforting arm about her shoulder and asked, 'What are you going to do?'

She choked back a sob and muttered, 'Why didn't I fall in love with you? It would have made life so much easier.'

Matt laughed shortly. 'I doubt it. Stephanides doesn't strike me as a man who would enjoy having his wife fall in love with another man. There's been no word from him, has there?' And when she shook her head he finished, 'You know you always have a home here, Amber.'

She nodded, and he went on, 'But I'm afraid this time you won't get away with fooling him.'

'I know. Oh God, Matt, I've made such a hash of everything! I've depended shamelessly on you. I was so afraid of him that I let everyone think that Nick was yours, and never even gave a thought to what it would do to your life.'

His arm about her shoulders tightened. He said quietly, 'I'd be happy enough to help you confuse the issue this time too——' His head jerked at a noise in the passage; the door slammed and Mrs Crawford's voice was cut off in mid-question.

Matt said evenly, 'This is my house, Stephanides.'

'And that is my wife.' Alex sounded bored, and very dangerous.

'And my cousin.'

Matt was not intimidated, but Amber stepped away from his sheltering arm. She looked at Alex, and although her reasoning self registered that he was in a towering fury, her emotional being could only see the tiredness behind his eyes and the bitter beauty of his face.

She asked, 'How long have you been travelling, Alex?'

The wide shoulders moved inthe slightest of shrugs, 'Twenty-four hours—it does not matter. I slept most of the time.'

'What are you doing here?'

He looked at her with such cold rage that she flinched. 'I came,' he said, 'to see if you were pregnant. That was to be my revenge, you see. To get you pregnant and then to take the child from you. But when we were in Auckland with your son I noticed that he has eyes the same as mine, as my mother's. A few other things made me curious. He has a way of looking from beneath his lashes and smiling which reminded me again of my mother. And you, my dear Amber, were very uneasy whenever I went too close to him.' He paused, but Amber was too frozen to move. She stood pale and still, her eyes wide open yet unseeing.

After a moment Alex went on, 'So I contacted my lawyer. He did a little research and told me of a new method of determining the father of a child.'

Harshly Matt objected, 'But that only proves that a man couldn't have fathered a child, not who the father is.'

Alex ignored him. Watching Amber with a stare which sent slivers of ice through her veins, he continued, 'This is an entirely new process which uses genes as a fingerprint. I do not pretend to understand it, but rest assured that the results will be accepted in any court in the world. It was easy enough to discover the information I needed, as everyone in the hospital in Auckland conveniently assumed that the child was mine. The tests proved quite conclusively that I am Nick's father.'

He paused, but Amber was unable to speak, her gaze fixed imploringly on his pitiless face. With contempt he said, 'I was not as surprised as perhaps I should have been. Everything conspired to warn me, from the surgeon's assumption that the boy was mine, to his name. You called him after my father, did you not? What do you plan to call the child, mine also, which you are carrying?'

Wearily, without hope, she said, 'Is there anything your spies can't rake up?'

He smiled, all surface charm and black menace. 'I suppose there must be some things, but as you know, money opens most doors. Money, or the threat of losing it. After all, you would not now be carrying my child if you had not wanted to save your lover's money.'

His skin pale beneath his tan, Matt demanded between his teeth, 'What did you say?'

Insolently Alex said, 'Did she not tell you? She would not have come with me except that I threatened to bankrupt you and see that you never found another livelihood.' He raked Matt's appalled face with a taunting regard, his voice stabbing, goading, as he finished, 'So how does it feel to know that a woman has prostituted herself for you?'

Matt ignored him, staring at Amber's white face. 'Is that true?'

She nodded, shamefaced, and he whispered, 'By God, I could kill you, you bastard!'

Amber called on her self-control and said quickly, 'No! No, I mean it! Matt, I should never have involved you in all this, this is nothing to do with you!'

Matt didn't even look at her. Gently he removed the hands that clutched at his arm and started towards Alex, his intentions plain. A small, sneering smile tugged at Alex's mouth; he watched, his lashes lowered, his hands cupped loosely at his sides. The silk had been torn away to reveal the dagger, naked and wickedly dangerous. It was plain that he was relishing the thought of a fight.

Aloud and with great fluency Amber cursed them for being so stupidly macho and, as they were clearly beyond reason, did the only thing she could think of. She gave a hoarse little moan and collapsed.

It worked; Alex sprang across the room to catch her, his long arms wrapping around her to lift her to the sofa.

Above her head he snapped, 'Get her something to drink,' but when Matt had left the room he concluded crisply, 'Come on, Amber, I know perfectly well that you are conscious. And so does your cousin.'

'Saving face,' she said, opening her eyes.

The fury in his face had died a little; he nodded, half smiling, cynical as the devil. 'As you say.'

But when Matt came back into the room Alex dragged her into the cage of his arms, binding her to him so that she could feel the thundering of her heart. He said harshly, 'She is mine. She called me to her and asked that I take her, not once but twice. Knowing this, do you still want her?'

'Do you?' asked Matt, not giving an inch.

Alex laughed, a ragged sound, bitter and harsh. 'I have

never stopped wanting her,' he said, as though the words were torn from his heart.

Matt said quite calmly, 'Then why don't you tell her so?'

Alex thrust her down on to the sofa, his hand touching her cheek in a gesture of total possession. Wide-eyed, scarcely believing that she understood him, Amber listened as he said, 'You can come back with me or not, on my terms, but whatever you do I intend to take the children. They are mine.'

'No,' she whispered. 'Not my children.'

He shook her, suddenly losing control completely. 'You did it to me, stole my child! You took your revenge, why should I not do the same?' Before she could answer he said in a voice roughened by the deepest anguish, 'For God's sake, Amber, how could you do it? How could you take my child from me, raise him to believe that another man is his father?'

Neither of them realised that Matt had left the room. Amber had known the truth would make Alex angry; what she had not expected was the raw pain she saw in his face.

'Not for revenge,' she protested, her voice shaken. 'Alex, it was because I couldn't bear the thought of him growing up to believe that just because he was a man he was a superior being.' She put out her hand, touching the hard line of his cheek, curling her hand along his jawline. 'Your stepmother—Irene—told me your father had a mistress, that all men did. My father . . .' Her voice trailed away, but she bit her lip and continued, 'I don't know how many times I saw my mother weep because my father thought so little of her and me that he couldn't be bothered with us. I was determined that no child of mine should grow up like that. You like women, yet you treat the women in your life as though they're witless! But it was never revenge. I didn't know I was pregnant until I'd been here for some months . . . And I've never told Nick that Matt is his father.'

'He must think so,' he sneered. 'He is not a baby, and he must know that you are lovers.'

She drew a deep, sobbing breath but held the fierce glitter of his eyes without flinching. 'I've never slept with Matt. He's my cousin, and I love him dearly, and I'd be stupid if I hadn't sometimes wondered what he's like as a lover, but I've never wanted him to be mine.'

The arms about her contracted fiercely, then jerked, and he threw her from him so hard that she cried out and fell awkwardly, coming down on her hip on the floor. Half winded, she lay there for a moment, trying to summon the strength to get up.

Alex was there, bending over her, lifting her, his expression appalled. 'What have I done?' he whispered. '*Pedhi mou*, have I hurt you?'

'No—oh, no. Only a little.'

He sat her down on the sofa and knelt on the floor in front of her, holding her cold hands in his warm ones. 'You do not have to lie to me,' he said gravely. 'I do not like the thought of your cousin as your lover, but I do not blame you if it was so.' His mouth twisted and she saw just how much he hated it, and saw too the acceptance etched there. 'I gave you no reason to be faithful,' he concluded harshly.

Amber shook her head and had to close her eyes against the fierce primeval pleasure burning in the depths of his eyes. 'He has never been my lover.'

'I should kill you for causing me so much pain,' he growled. 'Yet all I can think about is that there has been no man you love, no—— Has there been another man?'

She sighed. He had not changed that much. 'No, and what would you do if there had been?'

He leaned forward and kissed her eyelids. 'I would love you until you forgot that any other man had ever claimed a corner of your heart.'

Amber smiled, and at that moment the baby moved and she grabbed his hand and held it against her stomach, while Alex said something short and Greek under his breath, then said, 'Oh, my dear one, my sweet girl, can you ever forgive me for all the pain that I caused you? Can you live with me and love me and believe that from now on there will be only you in my heart, in my life?'

'Yes,' she said simply, and he laughed and bent his black head and kissed the place where his hand rested, then said, 'It seems to me that I am more fortunate than I have any right to be.'

She laughed too and hugged his head against her breasts. 'You always were, you've only just realised it.'

'Am I to believe that you love me? Even knowing that I planned to make you pregnant and take the child from you?'

Opening her eyes, Amber nodded, telling him quietly, 'You never even thought, as soon as you heard about Nick you took me to him. You couldn't have stolen our child away from me.'

'I thought I could,' he said unevenly. 'I was filled with black pride. It was the same pride which made me so unyielding over poor Gabrielle.'

She looked gravely at him, and he sighed and got to his feet and walked away across to the window. Staring out into the garden, swept by an autumn wind, he said in flat tones, 'You are a little unfair when you say that I think of women as toys. Perhaps it was so, but—it is hard to explain without making my father appear at fault.'

She said quickly, 'I know it's not fair to judge an earlier generation by our standards.'

His shoulders moved a little. 'I was his firstborn, his favourite. I loved him and I wanted to be the sort of man he admired.'

'Macho,' she said with a hint of mischief.

Alex sent her a crisp look. 'A word I hate, but yes, I suppose that is so. I grew up spoiled by my mother, waited on hand and foot and cossetted by every woman I met, and before I left school I knew that there were very few women I could not have if I wanted them. It was not good for my character. You called me arrogant. I am afraid you are correct.'

Amber smiled and leaned back against the sofa, relaxing bonelessly into the cushions while her eyes feasted on him.

'It was,' he said on a note of severity, 'very bad for me. But I was saved from the worst excesses of many young men in my position because my father made it quite clear that great things were expected of me.'

'And because you have a very strong character,' she said firmly.

He grinned, but sobered quickly and turned a little away. 'Perhaps. As for Gabrielle—at first I thought that there was no reason why I should not continue with her. As you say, in our society it was not unusual. And she was very—experienced, while you were sweet but innocent. However, I felt a little guilty at the thought—it seemed a poor way to start a marriage, with another woman in reserve, so to speak. And whatever I do, I like to do well, to give my whole mind to it. I did not want to believe I had grown so cynical that I was not prepared to devote the same determination to my marriage.'

Amber frowned. 'Then why——?'

'I felt guilty,' said Alex without expression. 'When I told her that as I was to marry I would not be seeing her again she wept, and I wondered if perhaps she had forgotten the rules she had always lived by and fallen a little in love with me. I was not her first lover, but we had been together for some time, to our mutual pleasure. So I did not make it imperative for her to leave her house, although she knew I would buy her one anywhere in France. Then two weeks before our wedding she came to me and told me that she was pregnant.'

'Poor woman!' Amber could feel compassion now. 'Of course you had to support her.'

He nodded and said bleakly, 'Yes. I wish I could tell you that I loved you then, but it would be a lie. I liked you—you were enchantingly shy, a sweet little thing with a mouth which flamed beneath mine—and I wanted you so much that I could not sleep for it. I suppose I knew that soon I would love you. And I am afraid I was very angry with Gabrielle, but I could not banish her—it was my child.'

'And you thought I'd never know,' Amber said understandingly.

His expression darkened. 'You *should* never have known. I would have cared for the child, loved it and supported it, and in time, when you had learned to love me and trust me, I would have told you.' He gave a smothered sigh and turned. 'I did not realise that it was not just your mouth that caught fire so easily, so quickly. That temper . . .! My stepmother wanted me to marry the daughter of her cousin. She was angry when I insisted on marrying you, and she became spiteful. She wished to punish me, so she told you about Gabrielle. But she did not mean to drive you away. I did that because I was arrogant and patronising—all the things you accused me of, and because I felt that in my father's house I should be man enough to control a child not yet eighteen. You were so defiant, so intransigent. I suppose I wanted you to be as lost in love with me as I was rapidly becoming with you.'

'In a way I was.' Amber paused, collecting her thoughts, then continued wryly, 'Not as I am now, of course. It was a childish love, a first love, but it would have grown. You speak of Gabrielle in the past. Is she not——?'

'No. After the baby died I took her to the South of France. She is now running a boutique in Cannes. I saw her two months ago, and she is very happy.'

'I'm glad,' she said simply.

Shaken, Alex came across to where she sat and pulled her up into his arms, holding her against him with reverence and a warm comfort. 'How can you love me after I kidnapped you? Do you not realise that I deliberately and coldbloodedly set out to break up what I thought was a long-standing affair with your cousin, whom I thought you loved? How can you love a man who would behave like that?'

Amber smoothed a tender hand over the frown between his brows, touched the hard exciting line of his mouth and whispered, 'Because I do. Because you were so wonderful when Nick was hurt. And although your upbringing, everything in that proud Greek soul of yours, must have rebelled at the thought of meeting the man you thought to be my lover, you stayed, you gave me support when I needed it. I don't seem to be able to resist you!'

He laughed at that, and kissed her, a swift hard kiss, and said joyously, 'Of course, my little heart. But now, tell me how it is that my son was born ten months and two weeks after the last time we made love.'

'Well, he was a fortnight overdue—Nick has always been one for doing things in his own time. And we made love the night before you left for New York, the night before I ran away. You were half-asleep.'

She reminded him of the occasion, and he grimaced and said drily, 'I thought it was a particularly vivid dream. I had had so many of them . . . Over the years, so many . . . and each time I woke and you were gone, and I knew that it was my stupidity, my blind arrogance which had driven you away.' He bent and rested his cheek on her head, gently, as if she was the rarest and most fragile creature he had ever seen. 'And then after his death I went through your father's papers and found the name of your cousin and wondered if perhaps you had fled here. I was—hopeful, excited, although I told myself that perhaps you no longer loved me. I was so conceited, in my heart I was sure that I could win you back. Because, I must admit, of all the women I have had in my arms, only with you do I lose myself completely.'

'Was that why you came up with such a mad scheme?'

He was smiling, she could hear it in his voice. 'You know me too well. When I received the reports from the firm of detectives I sent to watch you, and I realised that not only were you happy here, but you had a son, who was generally accepted to be Matt's, I felt betrayed. It was as though—as though we had shared a love so rare and precious that it was written in the annals, and you had dragged it through the slime. As though you had deliberately chosen to give him a son when you had not permitted yourself to get pregnant to me. I think for a while I was not sane. I decided to punish you, to take from you the one thing you wanted. You were a good mother; so, I would father a child on you and then take it from you.'

'I thought you were going to rape me,' said Amber a little shyly. 'But you didn't.'

'I thought I could, but it is not in me to treat a woman that way. I told myself that my revenge would be so much sweeter if you came to me of your own volition.'

'And was it?'

Alex said harshly, 'It was like embers in my heart, burning their way through my life. I sickened of what I was doing, but my black temper would not let me admit that I was behaving like a fool and the tyrant you called me. You were all that I had remembered—the sweetness, the joy was still there, but you had matured into an excitingly strong woman. To make you fall in love with me became a challenge—and one that I could not resist. It was not until I left you again that I realised that the greatest challenge of all would be to ensure that you stayed in love with me. But by then I was angry with you again. When I began to see small glimpses of my mother in Nikos, and realised that you were determined I should spend no time with him; you were like a cat on hot bricks, you hustled me away from him, and I began to wonder. The suspicion nearly ate me alive.'

Amber said softly, 'So that was why that last night you were so—so driven.'

He flung a haunted, fierce look at her, then turned his head away as if it hurt to remember. 'I was ashamed and angry and in pain—not a good combination. I had to go before I was weakened by this bitter love I had succumbed to. That last night—you were like a pagan wild and erotic, and I knew that if I wanted to keep my freedom I had to run away. But when I got the results of those tests and realised that Nikos is mine—I cannot tell you how angry I was then. I had not really believed that he could be, you know. I thought I was snatching at straws, that because I wanted him so much to be mine was seeing traits in him that were not really there. When the report from the detective agency suggested that you could be pregnant I was glad, because it gave me a reason to come back.'

Amber moved away and looked at him, read the self contempt etched into the strong features and said, 'To tell me you were going to take Nick and the baby?'

'That was what I told myself. But I think it was to ask you if there was not a chance that we could live together in happiness.' He essayed a smile, small and bleak. 'My schemes for vengeance had rebounded on me, because although I did not want to admit it, I had discovered truly how it was to love you, and lose you.'

Outside the wind blew a particularly heavy gust at the windows. The room was warm, but Amber shivered. 'And now?' she whispered. 'What happens now?'

Alex said confidently, 'We go home. And I will love you as if we have not wasted nine years of our lives, because in those nine years we both grew up, I think. And we will live happily ever after.'

It was the fierce barking of the dog which heralded the noise of the helicopter. Amber buttoned up her dress and smiled at the baby in her lap, rosy with repletion. 'Well, sweet Sophie, that sounds as if your daddy's home. Shall I keep you awake long enough for him to kiss you hello?'

At six months babies cannot talk, but they can smile, and Sophie had the same ruthlessly seductive smile as her father. She beamed at her mother and her step-grandmother, who had come into the room, and gazed around her with golden eyes as if expecting her father to appear from the walls.

Irene took her jealously from Amber's lap, cooing and smiling, her austere face oddly at peace. 'Go and meet him,' she urged. 'Nikos and Damon are already there, shouting and calling, little ruffians!'

Amber laughed. 'Little ruffians is an understatement!'

But she was glad that Nick had made the transference from New Zealand to Greece with so little trauma. He and Damon, the son of the gardener, were of an age and alike enough in temperament to become bosom friends, and after an initial awkwardness caused by the fact that Nick knew very little Greek and Damon no English, they got on like a house on fire.

She walked through the wide rooms, shaded from the sun of spring, and down through the gardens to the helicopter pad. Already Nick's voice was rising above the fading hum of the rotors; when Amber stepped out from the cool shade of a cypress he was running ahead of his father, shouting excitedly. Laughing, Amber moved aside to let the two boys race past, then waited until Alex came up to her, tall and formal in the dark business suit he had worn from Athens.

'Amber,' he said, and in her name was all that she ever wanted to hear.

She went willingly into his embrace, uncaring that Kostas saw; Alex had been away for three days and she was hungry for him, her slender body pliant against the hardness of his.

His mouth was fierce and demanding, but he cut the kiss short, lifting his head to laugh beneath his breath and say warningly, 'It is too public for what I have in mind. How are you?'

'Fine.'

'And the baby?'

Smiling, Amber moved out of his embrace and walked up towards the house beside him, telling him of Sophie's latest trick, enjoying his shout of laughter. When Alex came home the villa woke from somnolence, became charged with his energy. She felt the electricity fizzing in her blood, and to take her mind off the open response of her body, went on to inform him of Nick's latest exploits.

Later that night, in the big bedroom they shared, she came through from the bathroom wrapped in her robe and smiled at him as he lay reading in bed. 'I had a letter from Matt today,' she told him.

Alex put his book down and watched her as she sat down at the mirror and began to brush her hair.

'What did he have to say?'

She smiled. 'Nothing much. Reading between the lines, I gather that he's having trouble with the woman who's now his secretary.'

'Indeed?'

She smoothed the fiery fall of hair back from her face and got up. 'He said her work is good, but that he's having the devil's own job getting the men to do any work.'

'Indeed,' he returned drily. 'He should be accustomed to that. His last secretary was exceptionally beautiful also.'

His blatant appreciation still had the power to make her blush. Her colour deepened at his wicked chuckle, and she punished him by standing up and slowly peeling her wrap from her body, watching with pleasure as his eyes narrowed and the humour fled from his suddenly rigid features.

When he spoke again it was thickly. 'Are you tormenting me deliberately?'

For answer Amber tossed a laughing, teasing glance over her shoulder. He was out of the bed in an instant, the light falling in rose and copper over his magnificently aroused body, and before she had time to do more than squeak her surprise the wrap and the gold nightgown it hid were on the floor and she was on her back in the bed, with Alex poised threateningly over her. 'Say you're sorry,' he commanded.

Slowly, deliberately, she touched her tongue to her lip. 'Make me.'

Every time it was better. Every time she felt this melting heat through her body, when he was gentle, when he laughed with her, and when, like tonight, he showed her his strength and the power he had over her. Her breath caught in her throat; she met the blazing need in his face with a desire as intense, and surrendered to the flames of their passion.

Afterwards, silky with sweat, she lay half beneath him and ran an indolent finger from his ribs to his spine, not even thinking, her brain enveloped in a rosy, sated haze. Alex gave a small grunt of sheer contentment, and moved over on to his side, tucking her into his arms, his chin resting on the damp silk of her hair.

'I think,' he said in Greek, 'that I must be the luckiest man in the world.'

In the same language, speaking carefully, she returned, 'And I the luckiest woman. Incidentally,' reverting to English, 'your son informed me proudly that he can now swear in Greek. He was shocked to the core when I asked him how one swears in Greek. Women don't. Apparently this damned macho instinct is inborn!'

He chuckled lazily. 'Perhaps. Your accent is improving, my sweet one.'

'So it should be. No one here speaks anything but Greek to me!'

'It is the only way to learn.'

Amber laughed. 'I know, so I just might forgive you for giving them the order.'

He yawned, and stretched, but before Amber had time to react with her usual helpless excitement to the lean litheness of his body, he asked curtly, 'You are happy here? You do not miss New Zealand? Or England? I can move you to any place in this world, you know, if you find life too quiet or cut off here.'

She turned and kissed him softly, her mouth lingering over the high starkness of his cheekbones with loving delight. 'No, I like it here. Irene has forgiven me for marrying you; it's amazing what difference a couple of grandchildren make! We get on well now, and Nick is happy here. He gets a bit homesick, but he hasn't the time to indulge himself!' She moved sensuously against him and blew into his ear.

'Wanton,' he reproved, spoiling the censure by touching his tongue delicately to the corner of her mouth. 'And do you trust me now?'

He kept his voice light, his tone teasing, but she knew him well enough to discern the real meaning behind the question.

Very seriously, with all her love, she said, 'Yes, I do

trust you. I should never have thought you were the same as your father and mine. Even when you were refusing to give up Gabrielle, as I thought, you were unfailingly kind and gentle with me. I should have known then, because I doubt if my father was ever gentle with my mother, ever.'

'And my father believed very definitely that most women were the better for a harsh hand,' Alex agreed, adding very softly, 'But you were not to know, dearest, for I did not know then that the emotions which so confused me were love. I did not believe it existed except in romances. But now I know that where you are is home, and you are refreshment for my soul, and warm delight. Nothing, not casual sex with the most seductive woman in the world, or power or money, could ever give me the wild sweet madness I find in your arms. It took me long enough to learn that, but the lesson is well and truly committed to memory.'

Amber said in a shaken voice, 'In a way I'm glad we spent those years apart. I'm sorry you missed Nick's early years, I can never give you those back, but we grew up, both of us, while we were apart, didn't we? We learned what we really wanted from life.'

She could hear Alex's smile as he answered, 'And what was it that you wanted?'

Well, he deserved the surrender he wanted. He had matured over the years, but at heart he was all Greek, arrogant and jealous and autocratic. 'You,' she said simply. 'And my children But mostly you.'

'You fill my eyes and my heart and my life,' he said, and it was all the knowledge that Amber needed. As his hands moved tenderly, masterfully, over her skin she gave herself up to the sensual world he created anew for her each time they made love, and beneath the throbbing, pagan excitement, felt the rock-based peace that satisfied all her heart.

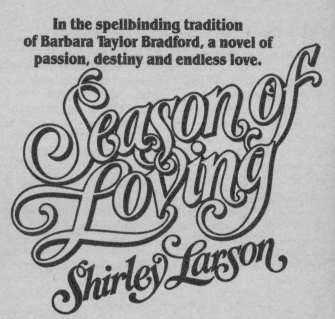

ATTRACTIVE, SPACE SAVING BOOK RACK

Display your most prized novels on this handsome and sturdy book rack. The hand-rubbed walnut finish will blend into your library decor with quiet elegance, providing a practical organizer for your favorite hard-or soft-covered books.

Only $9.95

Approximately 16" x 8" when assembled

Assembles in seconds!

To order, rush your name, address and zip code, along with a check or money order for $10.70* ($9.95 plus 75¢ postage and handling) payable to *Harlequin Reader Service*:

Harlequin Reader Service
Book Rack Offer
901 Fuhrmann Blvd.
P.O. Box 1396
Buffalo, NY 14269-1396

Offer not available in Canada.

BKR-1A

*New York and Iowa residents add appropriate sales tax.

Give in to Temptation! Harlequin Temptation

The story of a woman who knows her own mind, her own heart . . . and of the man who touches her, body and soul.

Intimate, sexy stories of today's woman—her troubles, her triumphs, her tears, her laughter.

And her ultimate commitment to love.

Four new titles each month—get 'em while they're hot. Available wherever paperbacks are sold. Temp-1

PAMELA BROWNING

...is fireworks on the green at the Fourth of July and prayers said around the Thanksgiving table. It is the dream of freedom realized in thousands of small towns across this great nation.

But mostly, the Heartland is its people. People who care about and help one another. People who cherish traditional values and give to their children the greatest gift, the gift of love.

American Romance presents HEARTLAND, an emotional trilogy about people whose memories, hopes and dreams are bound up in the acres they farm.

HEARTLAND...the story of America.

Don't miss these heartfelt stories: American Romance #237 SIMPLE GIFTS (March), #241 FLY AWAY (April), and #245 HARVEST HOME (May).